STATIC BETWEEN THE TREES

A HAUNTING COLLECTION OF UNSETTLING, ATMOSPHERIC SHORT STORIES

N.B. CROSS

NIMBUS BOOKS

Static Between the Trees

Copyright © 2025 by N.B. Cross

This is a work of fiction.

Names, characters, places, and incidents are either products of the author's imagination or are used fictitiously. Any resemblance to actual persons, living or dead, or real events is purely coincidental.

Published by Nimbus Books

ISBN: 978-1-970425-04-8

Cover Design and Interior Formatting: Nimbus Books

For those who still hear echoes in the quiet.

"I learned that just beneath the surface there's another world, and still different worlds as you dig deeper."
— David Lynch

CONTENTS

PART 1
WHERE THE EDGES BLUR

1 / WHILE THE SHADOWS
WAITED

At first, he thought the right side of his head had gone numb.

Kevin tried to lift his arm, just to press his fingertips to his temple, to check. But the movement was sluggish, like wading through wet concrete. His arm felt impossibly heavy, as if it belonged to someone else. It took everything he had just to raise it a few inches. When he looked down, he realized he was wearing thick gloves...industrial, padded. His head was encased in a helmet. A visor curved across his vision, tinted faint green.

This must be a dream, he thought.

That realization settled him. The fear of paralysis was dulled by the soft logic of dreams. The world felt submerged, but not in water. The liquid around him was denser...gummy, slow. Somewhere between syrup and jelly. It held him, embraced him. A luke-warm comfort flooded over him. He wasn't deep, maybe twenty feet below the surface. He could see light above.

He arched his back, craning his neck inside the helmet. Through the murk, shadows moved. People. Dozens of them. Walking briskly across the surface, as if the viscous sea he floated in were nothing more than frosted glass beneath their polished shoes. Businesspeople in slacks and skirts, high heels and briefcases, gliding forward with rehearsed purpose. Their faces were calm, their direction clear.

He recognized them. Or at least what they represented. The unspoken faked urgency. The carefully chosen detachment. The practiced indifference that allowed people to survive routine.

Kevin felt both kinship and sorrow.

Beneath him, only darkness. A green gradient that faded into pitch, untouched and unmoving. He tried to turn his body but couldn't. He was anchored by something—something he couldn't see, or maybe didn't need to see. Dreams didn't require explanations.

He could move forward, technically. But every step took him deeper, farther from the light. Walking backward did the same. So he stayed where he was, suspended in place. Caught in the stillness.

When he arched his back again, the scene had changed. The office crowd was gone.

Above him now was a spring afternoon. Children ran through a yard in white linen clothes, kicking a red ball between them. Their mother stood nearby, smiling. A patio table held a plate of cookies and sweating pitchers of juice. An overturned juice box bled into the concrete, drawing a gathering of ants. Laughter echoed down through the gel, distant and sweet. The sky was the soft blue of memory.

Kevin watched them for a long time. His eyes burned. He didn't blink.

When the vision faded and he looked back down, the gradient remained unchanged. Perfectly smooth. Perfectly dull. He squinted into the deep, hoping to see a shape, a crack, anything. But the void refused to offer even a mirage.

Time passed—though how long, he couldn't say. He began to sweat. Or maybe the water was warming around him. The green thickened into grey.

He bent forward, just to see something new.

Below him, the ground had changed. The gel was heavier here, almost solid. It pooled around his knees, a pedestal rising from the depths. Beyond it: nothing. An empty chasm that stretched forever. He leaned closer, felt the world tip beneath him, and straightened before he could fall.

A faint panic began to ripple beneath his calm. Not the panic of danger—but the panic of stillness. The kind that sets in when nothing moves, nothing changes. When you've spent a lifetime waiting for something else.

He arched his back again.

The vision above had reset.

The businesspeople were back, walking across a cracked sidewalk bordered by slush. It was morning. The sun was cold but bright. A robin pecked at the ground. A squirrel darted across a puddle. He watched the shoes pass —dress, leather, patent, sneakers. A blur of motion in a place where he could no longer move.

He blinked. The image remained. He closed his eyes for a moment longer, trying to will the dream into something else. It stayed the same.

When he looked down again, the green had faded entirely. It was grey now. Thick and heavy as wet cement. The pool around his boots had hardened. His feet were fused into the floor. He tried to lift one, but nothing moved.

A crack appeared across the visor. Thin at first. Then branching.

The pressure grew.

His legs were numb. His arms heavy. His chest couldn't rise the way it used to. The jelly had turned to stone. The world below was no longer an invitation—it was a tomb.

He tilted his head back again, one last time, aching for the spring field.

But it was gone.

Now, the yard was empty. The grass brittle. The ball deflated. Dry leaves scraped across the concrete. On the patio, an elderly woman sat in a wicker chair, sketchbook in her lap. A blanket covered her legs. She didn't look up. Her hand moved slowly, drawing something unseen.

Kevin stared at her. There was something in her posture. Something that looked like memory, or grief, or both. The way she held the pencil. The way she sat alone.

He tried to speak. His voice cracked in his throat. The world had gone quiet.

The green was gone. The grey was gone. Now there was only black.

He remembered his daughter's sixth birthday party, the one he missed because of a meeting that ran late. He remembered his son's voice on the phone, older than it should've been. He remembered the smell of early spring mornings, back when he thought there would always be time.

Above him, the old woman kept sketching.

He watched her until the black took that, too.

2 / STAIN BENEATH THE WALLPAPER

THE FIRST TIME they saw it, it was barely there. A smudge. The color of an old bruise, high on the far bedroom wall, where the ceiling dipped under the eaves.

"It's just moisture," the realtor said, offering a practiced smile. "The inspector didn't flag anything, and it's not soft to the touch."

Lena ran her hand along the wall anyway. Dry, she admitted. But there was something off about it. The shape was almost organic—an uneven oval, edges blurred like it had sunk in from somewhere behind the drywall.

Still, they signed the papers that week. They had both fallen for the bones of the house: arched doorways, creaking hardwood, a backyard thick with oak and pine. A real place to grow into. Maybe even raise a kid...someday.

They moved in on a warm Saturday in October. The smell of leaves drifted through open windows, mixing with the musk of old wood and paint. It wasn't until their second night there, after the boxes had been stacked in corners and the fridge was humming with promise, that they looked again at the stain.

It had changed.

Not much. But it looked darker now. Redder. Like blood through gauze.

Mark climbed on a chair to touch it.

"Still dry," he said. "But warm."

Lena didn't answer. She stood in the doorway, one arm crossed over her chest, the other resting just under her chin. Her mouth was slightly open, her expression unreadable.

They covered it with primer the next morning. Two coats, thick and even.

By dinnertime, it was back.

They tried to ignore it. People had lived in the house for decades. There were bound to be imperfections. Old houses breathed in strange ways, settled over time.

But the stain kept growing.

Not fast. Just enough to always be different. To make you question your memory. And it wasn't just the size—it was the shape. What started as a bruise became something more defined. Almost vascular. Like roots. Or veins.

Mark spent an evening online reading about mold remediation and wall parasites. He ordered a moisture meter. It came back normal. He drilled a test hole and shone a flashlight inside. No visible leak, no rodents. Nothing but insulation and shadow.

Still, it spread.

Lena picked out wallpaper. A heavy, antique floral with dark blue petals and twisting vines. Something that would feel deliberate, like a design choice, not desperation.

They spent the better part of Sunday hanging it. Mark cursed under his breath while Lena smoothed out bubbles with a plastic scraper. The paper had weight to it, made the room feel smaller but warmer. More finished.

That night, they drank wine in the living room and tried to forget what was underneath.

It held for three days.

On the fourth morning, Lena found the wallpaper bubbling. A single, raised oval, right where the stain had been. She pressed it gently with her finger.

It gave.

Not like damaged drywall. Not like paper torn from moisture.

It gave like skin.

She pulled her hand away quickly. Her finger was wet. No color. Just a thin, clear film. She washed it three times before she felt clean again.

That evening, Mark peeled the paper back and stared. The stain had come through again, larger than before. Its edges glistened. At its center was a dark knot, the size of a plum.

"Is that... a lump?" he said, voice hushed. "It looks... raised."

"It's growing," Lena whispered.

They didn't touch it after that.

The house changed around the stain.

The lights in the hallway started flickering. The floor near the bedroom door developed a soft give, as though something underneath had swollen. Mark tightened screws and replaced bulbs. He tore up floorboards and checked the crawlspace. No rot. No water damage. But the room felt wrong.

They started sleeping downstairs.

Mark joked about asbestos, black mold, some mystery gas. Lena stopped laughing at his jokes.

She spent more time in the bedroom. Sometimes he'd find her just standing there, staring at the wall. Her eyes wouldn't quite meet his when he asked her what she was doing.

"I think it's trying to tell me something," she said once.

He thought she was joking.

She wasn't.

One night, Lena stayed upstairs. Mark fell asleep on the couch, the TV still glowing. When he woke hours later, the house was silent.

Upstairs, the door to the bedroom was closed.

He pushed it open and stepped inside.

She was sitting on the bed, facing the wall. The stain pulsed, slow and steady. Like the rise and fall of a sleeping chest. Her hand rested flat against it.

"You feel it too now," she said, without turning around.

"Feel what?"

She didn't answer.

He backed out of the room and didn't go up again for three days.

A contractor came. He took one look and backed away.

"I'm not touching that," he said. "Whatever it is, it's beyond me."

They offered cash. He left the house without another word.

Mark tried tearing the wall out himself. He wore gloves and a respirator and attacked it with a crowbar.

He got one panel free before stopping.

Behind the drywall was no insulation. No studs. Just something red and slick and softly ridged, like muscle under skin. It flexed when he touched it.

He vomited in the bathroom and slept in the car that night.

When he checked the room the next day, the panel had been reabsorbed. As though it had never been removed.

Lena grew quiet.

She started keeping a journal, writing in it at night with the door locked. Her eyes looked heavy. Her voice was low and distant, as if coming from a few feet behind her body.

Mark tried to convince her to leave. To get out, just for a while.

She refused.

"He's not done with me yet," she said.

Mark left the house the next morning.

He drove three hours to his brother's place and didn't tell him why he came. Slept on the couch. Watched football. Pretended to laugh.

By the fourth night, he couldn't stop thinking about the way the wall had pulsed. The warmth of it. The pressure behind it.

He drove back just before midnight.

The front door was open. The porch light swayed in the wind.

Inside, the house was still.

Her journal was on the kitchen table.

The pages were filled with drawings. Loops and coils. Veins. A map of something that didn't belong in the world.

He went upstairs.

The bedroom door was gone.

Where the wall had been, the stain now stretched floor to ceiling, edge to edge. It rippled, slow and rhythmic, as if it had grown gills and learned to breathe.

At the center was the shape of a hand, pressed inward.

Fingers spread. Palm wide.

It was Lena's hand.

He stepped closer, lifted his own hand.

And felt it move.

Something shifted behind the wall. A response. As though it recognized him.

Welcomed him.

He backed away slowly, then faster. Down the stairs, out the door. Into the car.

He never went back.

The house was listed six months later. "Fixer-upper," the description read. "Old-world charm. Needs some TLC."

The wall was painted over.

The stain was gone.

But it still pulsed, just under the surface. Waiting.

The new owners were a young couple from out east. They liked the charm, the tucked-away street, the way the back-yard dipped into the tree line like a secret.

They painted the upstairs room first, eager to turn it into a nursery. The wall gave them trouble. No matter how carefully they applied the coat, the paint dried uneven there —always a shade darker than the rest.

They joked about it. Blamed the light, the brushes, the primer. They laughed in that way people do when some-thing feels off but not quite threatening.

Sometimes, late at night, the baby monitor picked up a low thrum. A kind of breath, steady and slow.

And once, when the child cried, it seemed to echo. Not through the house—but through the wall.

The couple never traced it. Never looked too close.

But sometimes, when the baby slept, they'd both stand in the hallway without meaning to. Listening.

Not to the cries.
To something deeper.
Something waiting to be heard.

Rumors of a party at the new kid's house spread through the school like a fever. Nobody really knew Tyler, but that wasn't a dealbreaker. The cheerleaders were going. That was enough for half the school. Sam, though, he only cared about Marie.

He pulled up in his Mazda pickup just after ten, the engine coughing once before falling silent. Humid night air clung to his skin the moment he stepped out, thick with the scent of honeysuckle and leftover sunlight. Summer was reclaiming the nights, and the edge of school felt like it was crumbling. That in-between time where anything might happen.

Boneheads congregated near the side fence, daring each other to leap over it like drunk gymnasts. One of them slipped and landed hard, groaning, while the others cackled. Sam walked past them and into the house, already feeling the pulse of music in his ribs.

Inside, it was a swarm of bodies, thumping bass, beer stench, and distant laughter. A shout from the living room—"Sam, you motherfucker! You need a beer!"—greeted him like a homecoming. He didn't say no. He wasn't much of a drinker, but parties had rules, and one of them was: never turn down the first beer.

The cup was warm. Already skunky. He wandered through the house, taking it in. Joe and Fiona were practically fused together on the couch. Mike and Bobby passed a paper towel tube stuffed with dryer sheets back and forth like it was a sacred relic. The room smelled like cheap weed and lemon-scented laundry.

Someone yelled "keg stand!" from the dining room, and there was Randy, upside down like an idiot, chugging foam while two football players anchored his legs. He never passed up a chance to be the center of attention.

Sam drifted away from the noise, toward the hallway lined with photographs. Dozens of them. Most were black-and-white. All were high school kids. Different outfits, different seasons, some mid-laugh, some looking directly into the lens like they knew what it could do. A couple of the faces seemed familiar, but none had names.

"Dude must have a lot of cousins," Sam muttered.

"Right?" said a voice behind him. It was like a needle in his spine. Not painful. Electric. Marie. She wore a tight blue shirt that hinted at the curve of her waist when she moved, her blonde curls catching the light like spun glass. Her voice made him forget what he'd just been thinking.

Before he could turn, a flash went off. *Click!* A bright pop from the living room.

"Say cheese!" Tyler's voice was too cheerful.

Sam blinked. "Come on, man. Do you have to do that?"

"Just me? Get one of us!" Marie said, stepping next to Sam and slipping her arm around his waist. Her hand was warm. Familiar. Sam felt his breath snag in his throat.

"Maybe later," Tyler said. Then he was gone, already melting back into the party like fog.

"You okay?" Sam asked her.

Marie shrugged. "He's... weird, right? Always has that camera. Kind of a creeper vibe." She held up her empty cup. "I'm dry. Think you could do the honors?"

Sam nodded, took her cup gently, letting his fingers trail across hers just a second longer than necessary. "Be right back."

He filled her drink carefully, trying not to spill any foam. On the way back, he paused when he saw Tyler snap another picture, this time of Randy, who was stumbling over his own feet and slurring something unintelligible to Jenna, the redhead cheer captain. Snap!

When he got back to where he'd left Marie, she was gone.

He checked the kitchen. Nothing. Outside? He stepped through the sliding glass door and was immediately hit by the quiet. Crickets chirped. Somewhere, frogs croaked in chorus. The house was still buzzing inside, but out here. It was almost peaceful.

"Over here, trouble."

She was on the trampoline, knees up, arms behind her head, looking like she belonged there more than anywhere else in the world.

He set her beer down on the picnic table and climbed up beside her. The springs groaned slightly under their weight.

"If you close your eyes," she said softly, "you can hear the chaos in there and the calm out here at the same time. Like two different worlds touching for a minute."

He listened. She was right.

They talked for what felt like hours. About everything:

school, parents, music, college, movies that made them cry but that they'd never admit to watching. At one point, their hands found each other and stayed. Sam forgot about everything else.

Eventually, his eyes grew heavy. He didn't even remember falling asleep.

He woke stiff and disoriented, back aching from the trampoline. The sun was up. Birds chirped somewhere too cheerfully. He sat up and rubbed his eyes.

The house was... pristine.

No red Solo cups. No cigarette butts. No dented beer cans. The yard was untouched, like no one had been there in days.

He stepped inside. The living room was sterile, staged like a model home in a new subdivision. No smoke smell. No music. No sign of life.

Three new photographs hung neatly on the wall.

Sam stared.

One was of a boy looking disoriented, mouth open, eyes wide with joy and confusion.

The second was a redhead with a wicked grin, leaning on a wall. A real knockout. Seemed familiar.

The third...

He stepped closer.

Blonde curls. Baby blue shirt. A smile that made his chest ache.

"Maria? Marie? Mary?"

He said it aloud, but it felt wrong.

He couldn't remember her last name either.

He tried to picture her face the night before. Trampoline, laughter, the feel of her hand in his, but it was blurring already, like a dream unraveling. He suddenly couldn't remember how they met. Or what she had said about college. Or if she had any siblings. His mind reached, but the memories were fading as he chased them.

"Let's go get some waffles," came a voice from the hall.

Tyler. Calm. Smiling. Holding that same old camera.

Sam turned to him, throat dry. "Who is this?" he pointed at the photo.

Tyler paused. "Oh, that's my cousin Marie. From Missouri."

Sam blinked. "I, I thought..."

"Would you like to meet her?" Tyler asked, adjusting the lens on his camera. The shutter clicked softly, even though he hadn't taken a photo.

Sam took a step back.

4 / STATIC BETWEEN THE
      TREES

EVERY SEPTEMBER, he took a solo trip into the woods. No phone. No watch. No company. Just a pack, his old radio, and the promise of silence. It was a ritual more than a retreat, something about the quiet let his thoughts reorganize, like puzzle pieces shaken into place.

He picked a different location every year. This time, it was a stretch of forest up north, where the trails weren't named and the trees leaned in close. It had rained the week before, and the map showed steep ravines and old fire roads that no longer connected to anything.

His wife stood on the porch with her arms crossed, trying not to look worried. "At least drop a pin next time," she said. "Even if you don't check your phone."

"I like not being found," he replied, smiling.

She didn't return it right away. "Just... come back."

"I always do."

Their daughter barreled out the door in socks, holding something small in her hand. "Daddy, wait!"

He knelt and caught her mid-leap. She wrapped her arms tight around his neck and pushed a stuffed bunny into his chest, frayed and missing one ear. "For your adventure," she said. "In case you get scared."

He kissed her head, breathing in the warmth of home. "I'll bring him back safe."

He tucked the bunny into the top pocket of his pack. It rode with him on the drive north, its single ear bobbing with each turn. The farther he got from the highway, the better he felt. Trees thickened, signs disappeared, and the last bars of cell service blinked away like stars before dawn.

By the time he reached the trailhead, the sky had softened into late morning. The trail into the backcountry curled like a loose thread into the woods, unspooling under his boots. A crisp chill hung in the air, the kind that only came after the first frost. He liked that part, when everything felt held in place, hushed but alive. He wasn't trying to escape anything. That's what he told himself, anyway.

He walked alone, pack snug, thermos clipped to the side. The radio he carried was a battered handheld model, his dad used to bring it with them on canoe trips when he was a boy. It rarely picked up anything anymore, but it gave him comfort. A relic from when the forest still felt bigger than the voices in his own head.

The first time he saw them, seven turkey vultures, they were perched silently in a birch tree, black masses against the pale bark. They didn't flinch when he passed. Didn't blink. They just watched.

The first time he heard it, he thought it was static.

click-pop-hiss

Then a voice. Crisp. Neutral. Like a weather report.

"He pauses at the fork in the trail, adjusts the strap on his right shoulder."

He stopped mid-step, blinking. A branch snapped somewhere off to the left. No one was there.

The radio hissed again.

"He continues down the eastern path."

He looked down. The trail did, in fact, split. East and west. He hadn't noticed it before. Chalk it up to coincidence. He shifted his strap, right shoulder, just like the voice said, and took the eastern trail.

A half mile later, he saw the vultures again. Same number, same silence. This time they were perched along a dead pine. One hopped down to a lower branch, heavy and hunched, and stared at him until he moved on.

The voice came back.

"He crouches to inspect the strange moss near the base of the cedar."

He crouched, halfway...then froze.

The cedar tree stood there, squat and knotted. And yes, some kind of mottled moss bled out from its base like a dark halo.

His breath caught in his throat. He stood slowly, eyes scanning for the source. No antenna. No campsite. Just pine needles and the dry chatter of branches.

The radio crackled again.

"He doesn't sleep tonight."

The sun was still high, but the words clung to him. He kept walking. Each bend in the trail felt sharper. Shadows stretched before they should've.

That night, he built a fire out of sheer habit. But he didn't sleep.

The vultures circled once above him, then settled in a tree nearby. Their silhouettes were jagged against the moonlight. Still. Watching.

"His bones are cold and aching, uncertain of how long he sat staring into the coals."

The voice was no longer neutral. It sounded like someone trying to impersonate neutrality. Too flat. Too precise.

He clicked the radio off. The voice continued anyway.

"He stands."

He didn't.

"He stands."

And then, despite himself, he stood.

Panic bloomed like fungus in the hollow of his chest. He threw the radio into the trees. It thunked against a trunk and vanished in the underbrush. Silence.

Then, from somewhere deeper in the woods, the voice returned, not through the radio, but whispered in the breeze like it rode on the air itself.

"He runs."

He didn't want to. He didn't mean to.

But his legs moved.

He ran until the woods blurred, until his lungs clawed at the air. Until his knees gave out and he collapsed against a tree, retching dry breaths.

"He cries."

"No," he said aloud.

"He cries," the voice repeated, softer now.

Tears came anyway.

He wandered, directionless. Moving to stay warm. Moving to stay sane. A smell of rot and wet bark hung heavy. Once, he looked up and saw the vultures watching from a rocky outcrop above. One lifted its wings but didn't fly.

He tried to think of his apartment. His job. His name.

The thought slipped.

"He forgets his last name," the voice said casually.

He laughed.

Except... he couldn't remember it.

Just like that, it was gone. Slipped through him like mist through a screen.

He shouted into the trees. "What do you want?"

No answer.

Then:

"He reaches the fire tower just after dusk."

A fire tower? He hadn't seen one on the map. But he found it. It rose like a splintered spine above the trees. The vultures were perched on the top railing, motionless. Waiting.

He climbed.

The stairs groaned. At the top, the world opened, no roads, no towns. Just forest, curling endlessly under a dimming sky.

An old radio console sat inside the lookout cabin, cracked and humming.

He didn't want to touch it.

"He turns the dial."

He didn't.

"He turns the dial."

A pause. Then:

"He *wants* to turn the dial."

His hand twitched.

He reached out and gripped the knob.

The dial moved.

The voice came through again, only this time, it was his own.

"He sees the figure at the base of the tower."

He backed away from the window. A shape was down there. Waiting. Not moving. Not quite a man.

"He watches it climb."

The stairs creaked once.

Then again.

He didn't look.

"He prepares to greet himself."

"What does that mean?" he whispered.

Silence.

Then a new sound, not words, but a rasping *beat* of wings. All seven vultures rose from the railing at once and vanished into the trees.

<hr>

The sky never shifted.

It remained dim and endless. It hung in that liminal, unchanging hue, neither dusk nor dawn, casting a light too flat to be real. The forest below blurred at the edges, soft and colorless, as if remembered rather than seen. The wind spoke in static, dragging threads of it through the trees, whispering nonsense, half-words, unfinished sentences. His thoughts circled like vultures themselves, wings wide, black shadows always just overhead.

He didn't know how long he had been in the tower. Hours. Days. Maybe he'd never truly arrived. Maybe he had been here before the hiking ever began. The voice no longer spoke in commands. It was quieter now, more like breath than speech, more like memory than warning.

"He lets go of the idea of being watched."

"He accepts the transmission."

"He becomes the signal."

The words had lost their shape, dissolving into his own thoughts until he couldn't tell whether he was remembering them or thinking them for the first time. Somewhere in the distance, maybe in his chest, he felt the dull ache of forgetting. His name. The trailhead. The last night he kissed his daughter goodnight. The way she had pressed the little bunny into his hand like it was a talisman, like it could keep him safe.

He curled tighter into himself, sitting with his back against the warped planks of the lookout floor. The air was dry and tasted faintly of ash. His fingers had gone numb. His breath moved in slow, shallow loops, and still the world around him refused to change.

Then something shifted.

Not a sound, exactly, more like a stillness interrupted. The air around him thickened. A quiet gathered behind him, low and full, like someone standing just beyond his sight.

He opened his eyes.

The stuffed bunny sat beside him.

Its one remaining ear drooped slightly, the other gone, just as it had been when his daughter gave it to him at the door. A smear of pine resin darkened its side, and bits of leaf and grit clung to its stitched paws. It hadn't been there before. He knew that. He hadn't unpacked it. Hadn't seen it since the first night.

And yet, it looked as though it had been waiting for him.

He stared, not breathing, not blinking.

Then, with a slow inevitability, he felt the faintest weight settle into the hollow of his palm. Soft. Worn. Familiar.

His fingers, without thought, closed around it.

The missing ear.

It was the last thing he felt.

Far below, the forest held its breath. Turkey vultures circled in a loose spiral above the tree line, silent and steady, as if watching for something they had seen before. A hiker emerged at the edge of the woods, brushing aside a tangle of ferns. He carried an old radio clipped to his belt.

It crackled.

"He pauses at the fork in the trail..."

NOAH STARTED WITH A SHOEBOX.

It wasn't much, a creased cardboard shell left behind after his mom's latest splurge at the outlet store. He cut a window into one side with the rusted kitchen scissors and folded construction paper into a crude loveseat. A rug made from felt scraps. A plastic bead for a lamp. It wasn't perfect, but it was his.

That night, while his parents screamed through opposite walls, Noah lay on his stomach and stared through the little window into the quiet room he'd made.

His father's voice boomed through the floorboards, slurred and stumbling. His mother's laughter, sharp and mirthless, followed like a clinking glass dropped into a sink.

Noah traced the edge of the tiny window with his fingertip, breathing slow. In the room, no one shouted. No one cried. The silence inside the box was clean.

His father wasn't always a monster. There were photos in the hallway: his dad in a flannel shirt, lifting Noah into the air above the leaf pile in their old backyard. But now the leaves were gone. The yard was just mud. And Dad mostly lived in the basement, slouched in front of the TV with a bottle of Beam tucked under his arm like a second spine.

His mom wasn't much better. After work, she curled on the couch with her phone and a glass of wine, scrolling for hours through other people's living rooms. Always smiling strangers in perfect kitchens, arms looped around glowing children who called them "best friend" in captions.

She told Noah to "go play" or "go outside" or "go do something creative." He had stopped asking for her attention long ago.

The second room came a week later.

Noah used an Amazon box his mother had tossed toward the recycling bin. He lined the inside with wallpaper torn from an old dollhouse book. A fireplace made from foam brick. A tiny paper plant in the corner. This one had a door, cut from thin balsa wood and fixed with a twist tie hinge.

Each night, he added a new detail. A book on the coffee table. A framed family photo (not of his own, but ones he cut from magazines). A knitted throw blanket made from old sock threads.

And when his real bedroom began to feel smaller, too cold, too sharp, too loud, he'd lay his head close to the second house and close his eyes. He could almost hear the hum of quiet electricity, the stillness breathing around him.

The first time a room appeared in real life, Noah thought he was dreaming.

He had fallen asleep in the attic, his secret place above the second floor, filled with forgotten luggage and dusty holiday bins. He woke in the middle of the night to find himself not in the attic at all, but sitting in a tiny parlor.

It was the same room he'd made from the Amazon box. The same rug, same loveseat, same twisted paper fern.

Except it wasn't a box. It was real. Life-sized.

And he was the only one in it.

He sat very still.

His breath clouded in the soft, still air of the room. It smelled faintly of glue and old books, just like the one in the attic. But now the windows had depth. They looked out into fog. The floor held his weight. The loveseat sighed when he sat down.

When he reached for the lamp, it lit with a quiet click.

He didn't question how he got there. Not at first.

Instead, he stretched his legs and rested his arms along the armrests. He closed his eyes. For the first time in months, he felt warm.

When he woke, he was back in the attic. The box was where he'd left it, but it was different now, warped slightly, like it had been left out in a storm. The walls were damp, the paper fern curled at the edges.

Noah didn't say anything. Not to his parents, not to anyone. But he started building again.

A kitchen this time, with a tile floor made from linoleum samples his mom had picked up and never used. A fridge fashioned from an old eyeglass case. He used foil for the sink and laid toothpicks across for counters.

He didn't decorate this room for anyone else. No family photos. No clutter. Only stillness.

The next time he found himself inside the room, it was the kitchen.

The air smelled like lemon cleaner. The surfaces gleamed. He padded barefoot across the tile, opened a cupboard, and found it empty.

He opened another. Empty.

No food. No dishes. Nothing but him.

Noah sat on the floor. He should've been frightened, but instead, he smiled.

At home, things got worse.

His dad punched a hole in the bathroom door. Then he left for three days and came back soaked in gin and silence.

His mom didn't notice. Or pretended not to. She talked more about herself now. About how hard it was raising a kid. About how "everything had changed" since she was young. Noah nodded at all the right times. He didn't listen.

He started eating less. Sleeping less. The world outside the rooms grew thinner.

He began making hallways, thin, narrow corridors that linked the other boxes. He glued them together late into the night. Built closets. Nooks. Reading alcoves. Guest rooms.

He added a second floor. Then a third.

He stopped going to school. His mom never asked why. Perhaps she didn't notice.

Instead, she muttered about the car needing tires and how the neighbors "never minded their own damn business."

She didn't notice the attic light glowed at strange hours. Or how her boxes vanished. Or how the basement, once cluttered with liquor boxes and old blankets, now sat strangely quiet.

Noah only left the attic to eat crackers or grab supplies.

Sometimes he'd wake up inside a new room. Sometimes he would be standing in a hallway he didn't remember making.

And once, only once, he tried to leave. He walked to the edge of the bedroom he'd built last week. There was a door there. He opened it.

But behind it was only more fog.

One night, his father burst into the attic, red-faced and shaking. He kicked over the boxes. Screamed something about "this trash" and "grow the hell up."

Noah said nothing. He just sat beside the wreckage, silent, as his father stomped away.

Later that night, a new room appeared.

This one had no door. No windows. Only a chair in the center and gray carpet on every wall. The kind of room you couldn't escape from, not really.

He didn't go inside. Not yet. But he left the light on.

Over time, he noticed he was seeing fewer people. Not just at home, where silence filled the gaps between TV commercials and the clink of empty wine bottles, but outside, too.

When he dared walk to the mailbox, the air shimmered strangely. Cars passed without drivers. Birds moved without flapping. The world had stopped noticing him.

Only the rooms remained.

And still, he built. He crafted a tiny courtyard with paper hedges and a dried-up fountain. A narrow library with a rolling ladder and blank books.

A sunroom with no sun.

He made a nursery. Not for a child. Just because he thought the rocking chair should have a place to rest.

One morning, Noah opened his eyes and didn't know which world he was in.

He stood inside a grand hallway, taller than any he'd ever built. The floor gleamed like polished obsidian. Shadows spilled across the ceiling like branches from trees that didn't exist.

Far down the hall, a door opened slowly.

A figure stepped through.

It had no face. No clear form. Just a silhouette, like something remembered wrong.

In its hands was something small and delicate: one of Noah's first pieces. The tiny felt rug from the original shoebox house.

It placed it gently at his feet. Then turned and vanished through a wall.

Noah knelt to pick it up. It was warm. Still smelled faintly of glue and childhood.

He realized then he hadn't spoken aloud in weeks. Maybe longer.

His voice felt like a stranger in his throat.

The rooms weren't just his refuge anymore. They were his map. His monument. His world.

They stretched in all directions now, up, down, sideways. Rooms inside of rooms. Some he remembered building. Others seemed to have built themselves.

Sometimes, when he walked the halls, he'd find a version of himself, smaller, younger, curled in a corner or tracing the lines of a window.

He never spoke to them. But he nodded.

They nodded back.

And one night, as fog pressed against every seam of this strange, private world, he found a final room.

It was simple. Familiar.

The same as his own childhood bedroom. The one he hadn't seen in months, maybe longer. His real one. With the peeling space wallpaper and the sagging twin mattress.

But everything was quieter now.

In the middle of the bed was a cardboard box. Inside it, a tiny version of every room he'd ever built. A perfect replica. Every hallway. Every rug. Every chair.

He lifted the box gently.

A single slip of paper rested at the bottom.

It read: **You are not forgotten.**

He sat down on the bed and held the box to his chest.

Outside, the fog thickened. But inside, everything was still.

PART 2
STRANGE ECHOES

"I saw my dad today," Tom said.

His wife didn't move at first, just blinked slowly and waited. She had learned not to interrupt these moments.

"I don't think it was him," Tom went on, his voice soft. "But the way he sat... it was the same. Same hunch. Same look on his face, like something behind his eyes was burning slow."

He looked down at his plate, untouched.

"He was eating Hardee's. Just sitting there on the edge of a planter, like he had nowhere to be. I couldn't stop watching him."

She reached across the table, warm fingers curling around his wrist. "You've been thinking about him a lot lately."

Tom nodded, but he wasn't with her anymore.

He was ten again, waiting at the edge of the woods behind their house, the silence full of buzzing things.

The wind danced through the poplars. He peeled the white bark from a birch tree in thin, curling ribbons. His stomach grumbled, hollow and sharp. He loved that stretch of time after school and before dinner—when the world still felt tilted in his favor.

Then: gravel popping. The black F-150 turned into the driveway, trailing dust. Tom ran toward it, leaping over tree roots and ducking under pine limbs, grinning wide.

He jumped onto the running board like he always did.

"Hit it, Daddio!" he shouted, banging on the door.

The tires spun loose. The engine howled. The smell of Hardee's filled the cab. Rick laughed, a sound like old radio static.

The tree came fast. Tom never saw it. His neck snapped clean. The examiner said he didn't feel a thing.

The casket stayed closed.

Rick served thirteen years.

He didn't speak at the hearing. He didn't fight the sentence.

He fasted every October on Tom's birthday and marked the wall with a single pencil line. By the time they paroled him, the wall looked like it had been clawed at by something quiet and hurting.

The prison gates opened like jaws. The world beyond looked wrong...too sharp, too fast.

Rick squinted into the light. Cars blurred. The sky felt bigger than he remembered.

"Take your time," the officer said. "Sometimes the air hits hard."

His ex-wife picked him up in a borrowed car. Her hair was grayer, her voice quieter. She spoke like someone reading a grocery list. She didn't ask questions, and he didn't offer answers. When he asked about their old friends, she gave him names like stones, heavy and short.

She dropped him off at a plain apartment with a

number instead of a name. She didn't turn off the engine. "I hope you settle in," she said.

Rick stood there for a long time after she drove away, holding the keys like something fragile.

The next morning, he started his job on a clean-out crew. A half-burned office building, not gone, but going.

Across the street stood a Hardee's. That struck him in the chest more than he expected.

He bought a sandwich. It was already cooling by the time he found a place to sit, a low planter, weathered, rim chipped on one side.

He sat and unwrapped the food, hands trembling more than he cared to admit.

That's when he looked up and saw the man.

Across the street, behind the dust-streaked office window, stood a figure. Mid-twenties, maybe. Still. Silent. Watching.

For a moment, Rick's heart stuttered.

He blinked.

The figure was gone.

"You're early," his foreman called from behind. "That's a good sign. I'll get the doors open. They shut this place up tight after the fire."

Rick nodded, though he wasn't sure he'd heard him.

He looked down at the sandwich again.

The grease had bled through the wrapper. The food was cold.

Still, he held it. Like something might warm if he just waited long enough.

HE WOKE to soft morning light bleeding through the curtains. The room was familiar, the pine headboard, the blue quilt, the soft whir of the ceiling fan...but he knew before he sat up that it wasn't his.

Not really.

The floor creaked in the wrong places as he padded toward the bathroom. The mirror reflected a version of him that was... off. His face was thinner. His hair grayer at the temples. There was a scar on his jawline he didn't remember earning.

Down the hallway, the kitchen smelled of coffee and burnt toast. She stood at the counter, humming. His wife.

But not.

She turned when she heard his footsteps. Same smile, same gold flecks in her hair catching the light...but her eyes.

Her eyes were the wrong shade of brown.

And when she said his name, *Mark*, it rang too high, too soft, like a note just slightly out of tune.

He kissed her on the forehead because he didn't know what else to do. Her skin was warm. Her body real. She smiled up at him like nothing was wrong, like this morning was any other morning.

He sat down and drank the coffee she poured him, pretending not to notice how the mug handle curved the wrong way, how the kitchen window faced the wrong stand of trees.

They talked about nothing. A grocery list. The neighbor's barking dog. She laughed at a joke he didn't remember telling.

And all the while, dread hollowed him out.

He wandered the house after breakfast. Every picture on the walls was wrong. Photos of vacations they hadn't taken, places they hadn't been. There was a framed picture of the two of them standing beside a lake he didn't recognize, his arm slung over her shoulders, her head tucked beneath his chin.

They looked so happy.

He touched the glass and felt something inside him break a little.

By noon, he went outside. The sky overhead stretched wide and blue, but even the color was wrong.

A thinner blue. A brittle blue.

Not the same sky he knew.

The trees along the street leaned at strange angles. The neighbors waved to him with faces he half-remembered but couldn't name. He walked until he reached a park he didn't recognize, sat on a bench beneath a rustling oak, and stared at the ground.

The day passed without him.

At sunset, he returned to the house-that-wasn't-his. She met him at the door, her face folding with concern.

"Rough day?" she asked, stroking his cheek like she knew every line of him.

He wanted to tell her the truth.

He wanted to say, *You're not her. None of this is mine.*

But when he opened his mouth, all that came out was a hollow laugh.

That night, they lay in bed, tangled together. Her head rested on his chest, her breathing soft and even.

He stared at the ceiling fan, spinning and spinning, trying to anchor himself to the sound.

In the dark, she whispered, "I love you, Mark."

He closed his eyes and let the tears slip out, quiet as breath.

He thought about the life he had lost, the one he could no longer touch, no longer even picture clearly.

The house that smelled different, the wife whose eyes were just a little darker, whose voice fell on his ear like the perfect chord.

The sky that was heavier, richer, layered with clouds he could almost reach up and touch.

This place would never be home.

No matter how much he wanted it to be.

No matter how kind she was, how warm the sheets, how familiar the rhythm of the days.

He drifted off to sleep as the fan spun overhead, carrying him further and further from a world that had already let him go.

LEAH WOKE to the sound of music trapped in a single broken note.

She sat up slowly, the couch beneath her damp with spilled beer and something sticky she didn't want to think about. Around her, the house was full of people, but no one moved. A boy with a Solo cup was frozen mid-laugh, mouth a perfect "O." A girl in a glittery dress teetered on one foot, hair swinging upward like a stopped pendulum. The lights overhead buzzed and flickered, casting long shadows that didn't quite match the frozen figures.

Leah rubbed her eyes, but nothing changed.

The world was caught, like a film paused on a frame no one remembered taking.

The windows were fogged so thick she couldn't see outside. Every pane glowed dimly, a pale smudge against the dark. She pushed herself to standing, the soles of her shoes peeling away from the sticky floor with faint, unpleasant sounds.

She stumbled toward the kitchen, brushing against the corner of a table. The surface rippled under her fingers, as if she had touched the skin of a pond. She recoiled, heart hammering, and checked the clock above the stove.

12:34.

The microwave blinked the same numbers. Her phone, when she pulled it from her pocket, said it too. 12:34, frozen, humming faintly as if trying to tick forward but unable.

"Hello?" Her voice came out small and brittle, swallowed by the heavy air. No one answered.

They just... stood there.

She moved to the nearest figure, a boy she recognized vaguely from math class. She touched his arm, half expecting him to flinch, to laugh, to snap out of it. His skin was warm, but he was stiff, like a mannequin wrapped in flesh.

Leah shook him once, harder than she meant to. Nothing. His eyes stared through her.

Panic tightened in her chest. She tried the front door. The knob turned, but the door wouldn't open, as if something had welded it shut from the other side. She pounded on it, kicked it, screamed into the heavy air, but there was no answer, no crack of daylight, no change.

The walls themselves seemed to sigh.

A subtle movement caught her eye: the wallpaper by the staircase fluttered, a ripple traveling through it as though the house were breathing. The floor dipped slightly under her feet, softening like wet sand.

The harder she fought, the more the world around her twisted.

She weaved her way through the still crowd, careful not to touch anyone. Every brush, every accidental graze of skin against skin, made the air thicken. The couch sagged lower into the floor. The paintings on the walls dripped at the edges, the smiling faces inside them smearing into blurred colors.

The static in the air grew louder, buzzing behind her teeth.

Then, through the wavering gloom, she saw her.

Maddie.

Leah's heart caught.

Maddie stood just past the kitchen doorway, holding a red plastic cup loosely in one hand, the other lifted in a frozen wave. Her face was turned slightly toward Leah, a smile ghosting across her lips. For a moment, Leah could almost believe she would blink, would laugh, would roll her eyes and say something stupid like, *"You gonna help clean up or what?"*

She ran to her, hope flaring.

"Maddie," Leah whispered. Her voice cracked.

She gripped her friend's shoulders and shook, lightly at first, then harder when Maddie didn't respond. Maddie was warm, real, but utterly immobile.

The air split with a soft crack, like a distant lightning strike. From the tear in the air, something spilled.

Memories.

The smell of wet grass after rain, clinging to their jeans as they sprawled on the hill behind Leah's house.

The endless summer afternoons, building forts out of couch cushions and twinkle lights.

Sneaking out to lie on the trampoline, counting stars, swearing they'd never drift apart.

The sharp, giddy laughter echoing off the quarry walls when they raced their bikes downhill.

The memories bled into the warped house around them, filling the sagging walls with colors too bright, too warm to be real. Leah could see it all — herself and Maddie at ten, at twelve, at fifteen, but the edges of the scenes blurred, colors running like wet ink. Faces smudged. Voices faded.

The floor pitched sharply. A cabinet door drooped open, spilling utensils in slow motion across the counter.

From the windows, something dark pressed against the fogged glass. A shape, indistinct but heavy, dragging long shadows across the white.

Leah gripped Maddie's hand. "Come on," she whispered. "We have to go."

Maddie's fingers remained limp. Her frozen smile dimmed slightly, like a lightbulb flickering on its last breath.

The house moaned again. Furniture leaned, frames toppled from the walls and hung mid-fall. The air shivered around Leah's shoulders, making her shudder.

If she pulled Maddie too hard, if she fought to drag her back, the whole crumbling world would tear apart.

Tears pricked Leah's eyes. She pressed her forehead to Maddie's, breathing in the faint scent of vanilla shampoo.

"I'm sorry," she said into the quiet. "I'm sorry, but I can't stay here."

The static eased for a moment. Maddie's lips twitched, just barely, the ghost of a smile returning. But her body remained still.

Leah drew back. Her fingers trembled.

She understood.

Maddie wasn't lost.

She was there, in every breath, every step forward through the mist.

The front door, when she tried it again, swung open with a reluctant creak.

Beyond it was nothing but mist... endless, slow-moving fog that swirled like river currents around her ankles. She hesitated in the threshold, feeling the pull of the fading house behind her.

She looked back once.

The living room was already sagging, the figures inside sinking into the soft floor, their colors bleeding away.

The music had gone silent.

Leah pressed a hand to her chest where the memories lived now... warm and pulsing, stubborn against the cold.

She stepped into the mist.

The door shut softly behind her, and the house faded into the fog, until it was nothing but a dream she barely remembered having.

In the pale silence, Leah kept walking, each step pulling her further from what had been, each breath filling with what remained.

The laughter, the promises, the soft summer nights. All of it fading.

But never gone.

Not while she remembered.

No stories of them exist, because no one who sees them remains to tell.

There was a time, though no one recalls it now, when a boy named Billy saw them.

He had been riding in the back seat of his parents' car, headed north to visit his grandmother in a town folded between old woods and colder winds. They'd just left a roadside restaurant, the kind with plastic booths and fading sun decals on the windows. The kind with food that clings to your hands long after. The last stretch of road was narrow, lonely. Pines leaned in close. The day had gone pale. The car smelled like French fries and paper napkins.

Billy didn't complain. He never really did. He was the kind of child who smiled at strangers and stayed close in parking lots. Church folks used to say he had an old soul, and that Jack, his father, seemed younger when he was around him. Those who saw them could tell that Jack really enjoyed his son. They'd often remarked on the way his father played with him, with a patience and joy that didn't seem rehearsed.

They crested a hill.

"Dad, what are those people doing there?"

Jack adjusted the rearview. "What people? I don't see anyone, buddy."

"There...at the edge of the trees."

Billy pressed his fingers to the glass. They stood just beyond the shoulder of the road—still as fence posts. Covered in a kind of colorless dust. Skin, clothes, faces all the same gray, like something left behind in a fire long gone cold. Not moving, yet impossibly aware.

He didn't want to see them again. But he looked. And when he turned, they were gone.

They vanished. Billy watched, neck strained, eyes wide. The road curved and the world moved forward. He didn't notice the thin column of smoke rising from where they had just been.

They arrived early.

"You made good time," Jack's mother said as she ushered them in. She had hair like fog and a voice that clung to old syllables. "Shepherd's pie just finished. Come in, get warm."

Jack took off his coat and looked around. The house was still. Familiar. The piano, the photographs, the faint scent of wood polish.

"You get new carpet?"

"Oh yes. That shag was impossible. Remember how you'd drive your little cars through it like snow trails?"

He did.

At the table, the pie was rich and steaming. Better than Jack remembered from his childhood.

They walked the trail behind the house after dinner. The orchard was young but eager. The trees bent under their own brightness, red and gold. A creek whispered nearby.

Susan curled up in the living room afterward, reading, blanket tucked under her chin. Jack did the dishes while his mother packed leftovers into mismatched containers.

"So," she said quietly, "when are you two going to give me some grandkids? I'm not getting any younger."

Jack blinked at the window above the sink, as if trying to remember something.

"We've talked about it," he said. "We're trying. But it's just us for now."

His mother gave a quiet nod and a slight grin. "Well, try harder.."

That night, as they settled into the guest room, Susan paused in the doorway. She ran her hand across the dresser.

"This room's always felt like it should be a nursery," she said, half-laughing. "Isn't that strange?"

Jack looked up from unpacking. "What do you mean?"

"I don't know. Nothing." She smiled and shook it off. "Just a thought."

She never saw it coming.

The coffee had just finished brewing. She poured two mugs. His the tall black one with the chip near the lip that she didn't like, hers with oat milk and cinnamon. It was Sunday, that soft, slowed hour when even the light seemed unsure of itself, filtering through the blinds in stiff golden stripes. She wore his hoodie, sleeves pulled over her hands, and the music playing low in the background was something they'd once danced to in the kitchen. She couldn't remember the name of the song, only the way he had smiled when he spun her.

He came out of the bedroom barefoot, hair mussed, lips set in a line.

She smiled without thinking. "I made yours the way you like it."

He didn't answer. He didn't touch the mug.

"I think we need to talk," he said.

It wasn't the words...it was the way he said them. Measured. Finished. Like a line rehearsed. He looked at the floor when he said it. Not at her.

"I thought we were okay," she said. "We've been tired, yeah. But that's normal, right?"

He shook his head. "It hasn't been normal in a long time."

Her throat tightened. "I don't understand. We were just making plans. You sent me that dumb meme last night. You kissed me before bed."

"I didn't want to ruin it."

"Ruin what?"

"The last night."

Her fingers tightened around the counter edge. "You planned this?"

"I didn't want to do it this way."

She waited for him to take it back. He always did. Even after fights, he'd come back into the room an hour later, arms open, that look on his face.

But not now. He moved toward the door, toward the small bag that hadn't been there an hour ago and slipped on his shoes.

"I love you," she said.

"I know," he replied. "But I don't think that's enough anymore."

When the door clicked shut, she stared at the untouched mug on the counter. The steam thinned into nothing. She didn't cry right away. She stood there for a long time, as if her body hadn't caught up to what had happened. Then her knees gave out, and she slid to the kitchen floor. Cold tile against her legs. The song still playing. Her hands shook. She pressed her palms flat against the floor, trying to ground herself in anything solid.

The silence stretched until even the walls seemed to hold their breath. After a while, she began to weep, her body motionless on the floor.

She opened her eyes.

The light through the blinds was the same. The same quiet hum of the radiator. The same softness in the bed beside her—still warm. She blinked.

No bruises on her knees. No empty coffee mug on the counter.

She rose slowly, the way someone tests the weight of a dream.

He was in the kitchen. She could hear him humming, off-key and unaware. The scent of coffee reached her before she reached him.

He smiled when he saw her. "Morning."

She stared at him.

"I think we need to talk," he said.

She looked around the apartment. It was almost exactly the same, but not quite. The couch was facing the wrong wall. A photo on the shelf had shifted; she could've sworn it was a picture of them, but now it was only her, standing alone in a park.

He stepped closer. "You okay?"

She turned and walked back down the hallway. The floorboards creaked in the wrong places. Her breath hitched. A thread of fear unfurled in her chest.

And when she closed her eyes, it was morning again.

She woke before the coffee.

The apartment was quiet in a way that felt too practiced. Staged. Like a memory reassembled from photographs. She sat on the edge of the bed and looked around. Her bedside lamp was a different shape now... taller, with a pleated shade, and the crack in the ceiling was gone.

She walked to the kitchen.

The couch had moved. It was under the window now.

The plant in the corner, the pothos she'd tended for three years, was missing. In its place, a chair she didn't recognize, woven and weathered like it had always been there.

He entered the room, rubbing his eyes. Same navy shirt. Same sleepy smile.

"You're up early," he said. "I was about to make coffee."

"You hate making coffee," she said absently.

He laughed. "What? No I don't."

But he did. Or he used to. Before.

She watched as he set the filter, measured grounds. Her mug, the one with the faded mountain print, was missing too. He handed her a new one, plain white.

She didn't drink from it.

"I think we need to talk," he said, just like before.

She said nothing.

"I don't think this is working," he continued, stepping into the rhythm.

She watched him say the lines like a man reciting from a script he didn't realize he held.

This time, she didn't cry.

She nodded once. "I know."

It startled him. His next line fell apart in his mouth.

She took the mug, forced a small sip, and left the room before he could say anything else.

The third time, she stood at the window long before he woke.

The glass was cold under her fingers. Outside, the sky was a dull slate. No birds. No wind. Just the stillness of a day that hadn't quite agreed to begin. Cedar trees blotted out any light that tried to reach the room.

Behind her, the apartment whispered.

The layout was almost correct...almost. But the walls felt farther apart. The hallway stretched too long. The kitchen counter curved inward like a crescent. And above the stove, a clock ticked in a slow, deliberate click. Not moving forward. Always the same tick.

She turned when she heard his footsteps.

"Morning," he said, tousled and bright. "Smells like rain."

There was no rain.

He set down two mugs. Both plain. No cinnamon, no oat milk. Just black.

"I think we need to talk."

She crossed her arms. "Then talk."

He blinked. "What?"

"Say it," she said. "Say the rest."

"I... I don't think this is working?"

"Why?"

He hesitated. "I don't know. I just... feel like it isn't."

He looked around, as if noticing the apartment for the first time. "I'm leaving you."

She stepped forward, close enough to see the flecks of color in his irises. She used to memorize them.

Her voice softened. "Do you ever wonder what happens after you walk out that door?"

"What?" He frowned. "Are you okay?"

"No."

He reached out, but she stepped away.

"I think I'm waking up," she whispered.

She stood in the kitchen long before he entered. The coffee pot was already full. The windows dripped with condensation, though it hadn't rained. A low hum hung in the air. Not electrical. Organic.

When she set the mugs down, one of them was chipped. Not on the rim. On the handle, like it had been dropped and glued back together.

She stared at the spot where the bookshelf should have been. Instead, there was a low cabinet, its doors bowed outward as if after years of frustration it had finally given up.

He stepped into the room, blinking sleep from his eyes. "Hey. You're up early."

He kissed her cheek, but she barely registered it.

"You okay?"

Silence. Accompanied by a faint smile.

He moved toward the coffee. She could tell his line was coming.

"I think we need to talk…"

A low buzzing interrupted him. They both paused.

A fat black housefly hovered between them. It struck the cabinet, bounced off, buzzed toward the ceiling light. He swatted at it instinctively, missed.

He looked embarrassed.

She just watched.

"I don't think this is working," he added quietly.

"I know," she said, calm and distant.

The fly was already there when she woke. Trapped between the blinds and the windowpane, tapping mindlessly against the glass.

She didn't open the blinds.

The hallway seemed narrower. The floorboards whispered beneath her feet, like something shifted behind the walls when she passed.

He was sitting at the kitchen table already, hands folded like a man about to pray.

"I think we need to talk," he said.

She met his eyes, calm and almost kind. "The light's different this morning."

He glanced toward the window. "Is it?"

She nodded. "Everything feels like it's already been said. Like the words are just hanging in the air, waiting to be spoken again."

He shifted, thrown off by her tone. "What are you talking about?"

She looked down at her hands. "Nothing. It's just a feeling."

He hesitated, as if trying to find his footing. "I don't know what's going on with you, but..."

A sudden *thwap*. The fly hit the side of his mug. Landed. Rubbed its legs together.

He flinched.

"Ugh, that thing's been here all morning," he muttered.

"I think it's always been here," she said.

She watched him squirm in the silence that followed.

She didn't bother to make coffee.

She sat on the floor, her back against the oven, knees drawn up. The apartment smelled faintly like citrus and burnt paper. The fly circled the room in slow, looping spirals. The buzzing came in waves. It grew louder, closer and then receded into the corners.

When he entered, he looked uneasy, like he'd been called into a room where he didn't know the rules.

"I think we need to talk," he said.

She looked at him, eyes soft. "Then talk."

He paused. The fly landed on his shoulder. He didn't notice.

"I don't know what happened to us," he said. "You're different."

She smiled faintly, almost like remembering a dream. "Maybe I've just stopped holding onto things that were already gone."

He opened a cabinet. Closed it. Opened the fridge. Stared inside like it might explain something.

"I feel like I'm forgetting something," he said.

The fly buzzed again, drifting lazily toward the window.

She rose slowly, walked across the room. "Not everything needs to be remembered."

He turned to her, searching.

She reached out, resting her hand against his chest.

"You'll get used to the quiet," she whispered.

She stood by the door before he could reach it.

This time, the kitchen felt hollowed out. The air had weight. The fly buzzed in long, uneven patterns across the ceiling, the sound echoing faintly like it had grown in size. It dipped lower, circled the light fixture. Its shadow danced across the wall like a second clock.

She wore her shoes already. A scarf tucked into her coat. She hadn't packed anything. There was nothing left to take.

He stepped into the room, stopping short when he saw her.

"Oh," he said, blinking. "Are you going somewhere?"

"I think we need to talk," she said.

He let out a short laugh. "Yeah. I was thinking..."

She pursed her lips and welled up. "I made you coffee."

He moved toward her, suddenly unsure. "You're acting like I did something wrong."

"You didn't. I needed some time."

"I don't understand."

"I know," she said, and her voice was kind. "But that's not your fault."

He opened his mouth, then closed it. His eyes flicked to the table, to the counter. No mugs. No coffee.

The buzzing grew louder. The fly hovered above the door, then crawling along the frame like it knew what came next.

"Can we sit?" he asked.

"It's best that I go now."

"Then what am I supposed to do?"

She looked around the apartment, at its melting familiarity, at the way the shadows leaned too far in, at the door that had always led to a hallway. Now, through the glass inset, she saw trees. Quiet and waiting. A forest at dawn. No path. No wind. Just stillness.

"Let it be over," she said.

He stared at her. "You're leaving me?"

She reached out and brushed a strand of hair from his forehead.

When she opened the door, the fly lifted from the wall and drifted toward her. It paused in the air between them, circling once.

Then, as she stepped outside, it turned and landed on the windowsill behind him.

He didn't move. He just stood in the center of the kitchen, a man left mid-sentence, surrounded by fading steam and quiet clocks.

She didn't look back.

The cedar trees closed around her like a breath drawn inward.

And for the first time, nothing reset.

PART 3
THE HOLLOWING

IT STILL PLAYS in my head like a loop. A flicker of sunlight through pine branches. The thrum of tires humming on pavement. The faint smell of fast food wrappers and winter air, dry and sharp. Sometimes it's louder. Sometimes I feel it in my chest, like it just happened. But it didn't. It's been years since the accident.

Caleb had come all the way down from school just to pick me up. That was the kind of brother he was. No complaints, no bribes. Just a "Be ready by noon," and he was there. His 2005 4Runner rumbled into the driveway like some beast. Our mom gave her usual warnings: No parties. No drinking. No wandering off with strangers. But she knew we weren't like that. Not really.

I was sixteen then. A junior in high school. And I was going to Winter Carnival at Lakenorth University.

The roads had been dry from the February sun. The kind that never warms your skin but still blinds you off the snowbanks. It glared as we moved north along Route 41. Somewhere past Fossel Hollow, we stopped for gas. The place was a clapboard box squatting beside the road, half-buried in drifts. Caleb went in to use the bathroom. I stayed by the chip rack, trying to look casual while a kid behind the counter stared at me too long.

He was maybe my age, maybe older, with bad skin and a blank expression like he wasn't even seeing me.

"Did you see that guy?" I said when Caleb came back. "Creepy. Shouldn't he be in school?"

Caleb laughed — a two-toned chuckle I'd heard since childhood. "You've never been up in the Huron stretch before," he said. "Things get weird up here. Whole different rhythm. You start to hear banjos."

He grinned at me like I wouldn't get the joke, but I did.

"So, like… is that what Lakenorth students are like?"

He made a face. "No. No. We're normal. Mostly. I mean… you gotta be sharp to make it. It's all engineering and applied stuff. No room for fluff."

He didn't say it, but I knew he was proud. Sophomore year and he hadn't flunked out. He never had much discipline back home — I used to catch him "studying" with a game controller in one hand and Faith No More blasting from his room. But something had clicked when he got away. I admired him for that. I wanted to say so, but I never did.

The deer came out of nowhere. I barely got the words out.

"Cay! Watch out!"

One bound over the guardrail and we were in it. He'd told me once, years before, that it's better to hit a deer than to swerve. So he hit it. Straight on. But we were on the dark side of Ridgehill. The shade kept the ice there long after the sun burned it off elsewhere. The moment the tires struck the ice, we started to spin.

We weren't going fast, but fast enough. When the wheels caught dry pavement again, we flipped. The 4Runner slammed the guardrail, then tumbled through brush and down into the trees. It all happened in flashes. Pines. Sky. Pines. Sky. The truck folded into a maple trunk. The sound was like metal screaming.

Then it was just stillness.

I remember the blood. The needles in my hair. The windshield fractured like ice in a pond. I couldn't move. My legs were pinned. My arms too. Caleb's airbag had gone off. His head was tilted at a strange angle, like a puppet whose strings were cut.

"Caleb..." I tried to whisper. My voice came out hollow, like someone else's. I wanted to reach for him, just brush his sleeve or hold his hand. But I couldn't. I was cold and burning at the same time. Then sirens. Then nothing.

I wake in moments now. Or I think I do. It's hard to tell how much time has passed. The hill looks the same, though sometimes I sense the trees have changed shape. A sapling grows. A branch rots and falls. Moss creeps across stone.

I remember what they said. The papers called it a miracle. That he survived at all. That someone found us. That help came quickly. But I didn't want that miracle. I wanted to stay with him. I wanted cocoa in a mug too hot to hold. I wanted to walk through snow sculptures with him. Meet his friends. Sit awkwardly in someone's dorm room while people played bad music and drank cheap beer. Maybe flirt. Just a little.

Instead, I'm here.

I don't know what I am now. I don't feel the cold, but I notice it. I don't cast a shadow. Sometimes animals notice me. Sometimes they don't. Time moves differently. Days blur. Some nights I hear tires hissing in the snow or the low hum of music passing through closed windows. I watch. Always watch.

When I see a 4Runner, my chest flutters for a moment. But it's never him. Different headlights. Different music. Sometimes couples. Sometimes families. Once, I saw a kid who reminded me of me. I wanted to reach out. But I can't.

They paved a memorial into the bend. There's a cross nailed to a pine. Plastic flowers. Sometimes real ones, though they don't last. Once, someone left a photo. It was Caleb. In his Lakenorth hoodie, smiling with his arm around a girl I didn't know. I stared at it for hours. I wanted to hate her, but I didn't. I just wished it could've been me in the photo with him, even if just for that day.

There's not much wind here, but it still finds a way to whisper. I used to think it was my imagination, but I know better now. It's memory, echoing back. I still hear Caleb laughing. I still hear his voice telling me about classes, or music, or his weird roommate who showered at midnight and sang old blues songs.

I think the world forgets us eventually. People stop driving this way. The school might close someday. Caleb will graduate, move away. I hope he forgets this hill. I hope he doesn't carry guilt. I hope he becomes exactly who he was supposed to be. I hope he never looks back.

But still.

Still I wait.

Every once in a while, I swear I see him. Almost ust as he was. Just... a shape in a car. Singing with the window down. Hair tousled, eyes bright. Maybe it's a trick. Maybe it's just longing wearing a familiar face.

But if I could have one wish...not to live again, not to be remembered, not even to move on, it would be to see him one last time. Really see him. And maybe he'd slow down. Maybe he'd roll down his window. Maybe he'd know I was here.

Maybe he'd stop.

Just long enough to say goodbye.

The lagoon used to be a good place to fish.

It wasn't much to look at now. Overgrown. Shallow in most places. The reeds had crept in like slow, quiet invaders, and a few old boards from the dock still jutted out crooked from the mud. But back then...when the mornings felt colder and the days seemed longer, it had been the best kind of secret. The kind that belonged to their dad, and by extension, to them.

Josh remembered what it was like to be woken in the blue-gray hush of early morning. No birds yet. No traffic. Just the sound of their dad moving through the kitchen downstairs, and the creak of floorboards as he tried not to wake their mom.

Josh would bury his face in the pillow, trying to pretend he was still asleep. But Ed was already up. He was always up. Pulling jeans over pajama shorts, jostling Josh with an elbow or a whisper. "Come on. He's already got the Scout packed."

Josh hated getting up that early. Hated the cold floor, the scratchy layers of flannel, the rush to leave before the sun came up. He hated missing Saturday morning cartoons, especially the good ones that came on before nine. He'd grumble, drag his feet, but eventually he'd get his boots on and follow his brother out to the truck.

The old International Scout sat rumbling in the driveway, its windows already fogged from the inside. Their dad gave a nod, handed them a paper bag of donuts. Sugar-coated, still warm. A peace offering. Josh climbed into the back seat, still half-asleep, curling around the tackle box.

The drive felt longer than it probably was. A winding road through foggy stretches of pine, a dirt turnoff, and then the path down to the shore. The boat was kept hidden in the tall grass, a dinged-up pram that smelled like varnish and damp rope. Josh remembered helping drag it through the reeds, though he was never very much help. His boots stuck in the muck, and more than once he nearly fell in. Ed pushed from the back while their dad steadied the front. Eventually, they got it to the edge and loaded the supplies: oars, cooler, tin of cookies, thermos of coffee.

When the pram finally slid into the water, Josh always felt a small twinge of wonder. The world seemed quieter once they were afloat, as if sound didn't travel the same way over the water. Their dad rowed to the deep spot. He always said that was where the biggest fish waited, patient and ancient, just above the silt and shadows. Josh didn't care about the deep spot. He didn't care about fishing at all.

He sat with the pole in his hands, legs tucked under him, watching the worm on his hook disappear below the surface. He hated the smell. Hated the way the line felt too light in his hands. But the snacks were good: homemade chocolate chip cookies, a bag of red licorice for each of them, and the occasional bottle of Redpop, ice-cold from the cooler.

"Josh, don't let your pole rub on the side," his dad would say. "Scares the fish."

Josh always forgot. He spent most of the time daydreaming, thinking about what cartoons he was missing, what toys he might buy if they stopped at the hardware store afterward. Once, as he sat lost in thought, he felt a tug on his line. He panicked, jerked it just like his dad told him and launched the fish in a perfect arc right over the boat.

It smacked the water behind them and disappeared again, but their dad laughed. Really laughed. Slapped his knee and said, "That's how you do it!"

Josh smiled now, remembering that moment. That laugh. He hadn't heard it in a long time.

Josh crouched beside the water, watching the rippleless surface reflect the low clouds overhead. The lagoon was smaller now. Narrower. Choked by tall grass and cattails. But the deep spot was still there, just barely. A dark eye of water staring up from the past.

He unscrewed the metal cap of the small urn. The wind picked up, tugging at his shirt. For a moment he held the ashes close, unsure if it was too breezy. Unsure if he was ready.

"You hated fishing," Ed had told him over the phone. "Why there?"

Josh didn't know how to explain it. That it wasn't about fishing. It was about their dad waking them before the sun. The way his voice changed when he was on the water... softer, less clipped. The smell of the plastic tackle box, the rattle of lures. The silence, too. A silence that never felt empty.

There weren't many mornings like that. Their dad worked a lot, and when he was home, he wasn't always easy. But out on that little boat, it was different. He told stories.

Taught them to tie knots. Asked them about school. And even though Josh had hated fishing, he'd loved the sound of his dad's voice telling them which lure to use, or how the mist on the water meant a good catch.

He sat down on one of the flat rocks, setting the urn beside him.

The cookies had always come in a tin with a faded image of Santa Claus on the lid, even in July. Their mom made a batch the night before, and Josh always reached for the ones with the burnt edges. Ed would trade him those for the soft, middle ones. And the licorice, red ropes, two for each of them. His dad never took any, just sipped black coffee from an old green thermos, the lid doubling as a cup.

Josh pulled out a single piece of licorice from his jacket pocket. He'd found a pack at the gas station on the way in. It wasn't the same brand, but the gesture felt right. He broke it in half and tossed one piece into the water. It floated for a moment before sinking slowly, a red thread slipping out of view.

A heron lifted from the reeds with a sudden flap. Its wings cast a brief shadow over the water, then it disappeared behind the pine trees.

Josh exhaled.

When they were younger, Ed always caught more fish. He had the patience for it. Josh had preferred to watch the dragonflies dart between lily pads. To squint at the way the sun cracked the surface of the lake into gold slivers. He'd lay back in the boat sometimes, feet tucked under him, listening to the creak of the oars and the quiet plunk of line hitting the water.

It had taken him years to realize how much those mornings meant.

Josh reached for the urn again and opened it. He held it

over the water and let the ashes slip free, a slow, silty stream into the deep spot.

"Bye, Dad," he said.

The breeze picked up again, but not enough to scatter anything. Just enough to curl the last of it into the air and then let it settle.

He sat there a long time. Until the clouds broke a little. Until the water stilled again. And then, before he stood up to leave, he leaned over and whispered something only the lake would hear.

"Next time, I'll bring the cookies."

Josh stayed by the water for a while. Long enough for the sun to shift behind a mess of slow-moving clouds. Long enough for the wind to die down.

Eventually, he stood. His knees cracked a little as he straightened. He brushed the dirt off his jeans and slipped the now-empty urn back into his backpack.

The walk to the car was quieter than before. The reeds rustled less. Even the birds seemed to have wandered off. He followed the old path, careful on the uneven rocks. His boots left faint marks in the damp mud, but even those would be gone by morning.

Halfway up the trail, he paused near a birch tree, thin, white, peeling bark like dry skin curling at the edges. Hovering just off the mossy stump beside the trail: a dragon-fly. Its wings caught the light, flickering like silver thread. It hovered in place for a moment, twitching in the air, then darted away with no sound at all.

Josh watched it disappear into the trees.

His son had no interest in fishing. Not yet, anyway. Josh had tried once, suggesting a trip out to the river with poles and a tackle box, but the boy had shrugged, too caught up in a screen to look up. Josh hadn't pushed. He remembered what that was like, being small and disinterested, always thinking you knew better.

But maybe one day, he thought. Maybe they'd try again.

The Scout was long gone, but his sedan sat waiting at the trailhead, dusted with pollen and tree fluff. He dropped his pack in the trunk and slid into the driver's seat. Sat there a minute without turning the key. The trees stood silent, casting long shadows. A few, he thought, had grown older with him, seeming to nod at the passing of another wayfaring soul.

He looked once more toward the path, just a faint line now under the trees.

And then he started the car, put it in drive, and rolled slowly away.

THE SOUND CAME JUST after dawn.

A low, splintering crack...like ice giving way underfoot, or a tree breaking somewhere deep in the woods where no one had walked in years. It rolled through the air, low and wide, and then vanished. Not a bang. Not a rumble. Just a sound. Then silence.

Hazel Cartwright paused on her front step, holding a chipped mug of coffee to her chest. She squinted toward the sky. Pale blue, streaked with high, harmless clouds. No sign of a storm. The trees didn't stir.

"Sounded like it came from the ridge," she muttered, to no one.

Across the street, Carl Juneau stepped out to feed his chickens. He raised a hand to Hazel. "You hear that just now?"

She nodded. "Crack like a tree snapping."

"Sky didn't look right just before. Kinda... stretched." Carl frowned. "Could be nothing."

It was never nothing in Cornell. In a town of barely 600, people noticed when the wind changed direction, when the Miller boy skipped school, when the smell from the tannery shifted west. Hazel waited a few minutes longer on her porch. The sky held still. No one else seemed to be rushing out with news.

She went back inside, switched on the radio. Static. No music. She twisted the dial. Every station the same. Just static, soft and low, like breath in a dark room.

Hazel set her coffee down, hand hovering over the radio knobs. She wasn't the panicking kind. Not anymore. Not since Pete died. There were bigger things in life than a broken signal or a strange noise.

Still, she kept the radio on as she dressed.

Down the road, three houses west, Georgia and Vince Sandlin were sitting down to breakfast. Vince buttered toast for both of them the way he had every morning for the last thirty-eight years. Georgia was humming, low and tuneless, like she always did when the morning felt odd.

"You feel it too?" Vince asked, not looking up.

Georgia nodded, stirring her tea. "Something cracked open."

He didn't ask what she meant. Neither of them did, not anymore. You get to a certain age, and you learn when not to speak a thing into existence.

Hazel drove to town slow, gravel popping under the tires of her old Buick. Main Street looked the same as it always did: a line of brick storefronts, two faded crosswalks, and a stoplight that had been blinking yellow since the county budget ran dry last spring.

She parked in front of the post office and walked to the diner instead. She didn't have mail to send. She just wanted to see who else had heard it.

Inside, the smell of burnt bacon and dish soap clung to the walls. Linda Krawczak, the waitress with the stained apron and a short fuse, poured Hazel a cup before she asked for it.

"You hear that noise this morning?" Hazel asked, settling into a booth.

Linda nodded, but didn't say anything.

From behind the counter, Warren Kray cleared his throat. "You mean that splitting sound?" He was in his eighties, still came in every morning with his wife's picture folded in his wallet like a pressed flower. "Like something tearing down the middle."

Hazel looked around. A few others nodded.

"It wasn't thunder," someone said.

"It wasn't wind either," said another.

Linda finally spoke. "Radio's been out. Every station. Just static."

Hazel's stomach turned a little at that. "Mine too."

Warren looked down at his coffee, hands shaking faintly. "You think something's happened?"

Hazel didn't answer. Nobody did.

A bell rang above the door. Everyone looked up, but it was just June Carter, the mechanic's wife, with her youngest in tow. She looked pale, distracted. Sat down and didn't speak to anyone.

Hazel leaned over the table. "You alright, June?"

June looked up like she was trying to remember what question had been asked. "Have you seen my sister this morning?"

Hazel shook her head. "No, I thought she worked mornings at the pharmacy."

"She does," June said. "But she wasn't there when I stopped by. Place was locked."

The boy beside her reached for a sugar packet and tore it open too fast. White granules spilled across the table.

"Maybe she's late," Hazel said gently.

June nodded, but her eyes didn't settle.

Outside, the wind picked up. The sky shifted. Not darker, exactly—just thinner. Hazel felt it, the way you feel heat before a fever sets in.

Something was happening. Not loud. Not dramatic.

But something was breaking.

The town wasn't quick to panic.

People here were used to outages, blizzards, things not going according to plan. But by late afternoon, June was still asking about her sister. Not just in the diner. She went door to door.

Her sister's name was Marcy.

Marcy, who stocked cough drops at the pharmacy and hand-wrote birthday cards for customers she liked. Marcy, who made sun tea on her back porch and owned a red windbreaker everyone in town recognized. No one had seen the jacket. No one had seen her.

Her house was locked. Car still in the drive.

Sheriff Delaney came out in his brown cruiser and took a look around. Didn't find anything out of place. Said she probably left town for the day, maybe to visit her cousin in Traverse.

"She didn't say anything about leaving," June kept saying. "She'd never leave without telling me."

Delaney made a note in his pad and told her to check back tomorrow. "People drift sometimes," he said, like that was a comfort.

But people didn't drift here. People got stuck, rooted like old fence posts in clay. You didn't leave without someone knowing, without someone spotting you at the gas station or the junction. That's how it had always been.

That night, Hazel sat on her porch with the radio playing low. Static still.

She watched the stars come out and thought about the crack in the sky.

Something had come through. She could feel it. Like wind through a split pane.

The next morning, there were three missing.

Marcy.

The Henderson boy: Eli, twelve years old, last seen riding his bike near the river.

And Margaret Dwyer: who lived above the barber shop and hadn't been seen since the day before yesterday, though no one had noticed until now.

People gathered in the church basement. Sheriff Delaney stood in front of the chalkboard usually used for Sunday school. He looked uncomfortable, out of place without a podium.

"This is likely a coincidence," he began. "One person leaves, another doesn't come home, maybe they're together..."

"No," said June. She was in the front row, arms crossed. "Marcy wouldn't run."

"Eli's bike was still in the garage," his father added. "Tires full. Helmet on the hook."

From the back, Linda raised a hand. "What about the sound?"

Delaney blinked. "What sound?"

"That split, cracking sound."

A dozen voices murmured in agreement. Someone mimicked it aloud—krrk—and people nodded.

The sheriff hesitated, then wrote a single word on the chalkboard:

CRACK

Hazel watched the word and felt the skin on her arms prickle. It wasn't the sound itself that unnerved her. It was how everyone heard it, and how no one could say what it was.

No storm. No explosion. No skyward flash.

Just a rift.

Hazel didn't sleep that night.

She kept the porch light on and the curtains cracked, as if Marcy or the Henderson boy might come up the driveway needing help. But no one came. The radio still whispered static when she turned it on. It was starting to feel personal. Like something watching her breathe.

She went to the store the next morning and noticed the shelves hadn't been restocked. Fred, the owner, was gone. His wife stood behind the register, trembling, trying to run the till with shaking hands.

"He didn't come home," she said quietly. "Left for the lake yesterday morning to fish. Never came back."

Hazel bought canned beans and toothpaste, even though she had both at home. She didn't want to leave the store too fast. Didn't want to go back to an empty house.

Outside, the town felt quieter than usual. Not peaceful. Just... vacant. Like the spaces people used to occupy were still shaped around them, but they'd been pulled out of their outlines.

She drove out toward the ridge. She didn't know why, not really. Just felt like she should go where the sound had come from. The road curved through thinning trees, brittle grass swaying in the wind. The air smelled metallic.

She parked by the old overlook and stepped out.

Silence. The kind that presses against your eardrums. The kind that makes you doubt your own heartbeat.

Hazel stood there a long while. Waiting, maybe, for a second crack. A clue. Anything.

Nothing came.

Just the same sky. A little too pale. A little too thin.

Back home, she found a note in her mailbox.

Not a letter. Not handwritten. Just a single page, typed, with no return address.

I saw something in the mirror that wasn't me.

That was all it said.

No signature. No context. Hazel stared at it on the kitchen table while the wind rattled the storm windows.

She tried to call the sheriff. No signal.

She tried to call her son in Ironwood. Static.

Tried to call the diner. Nothing.

By evening, the lights flickered. Then held. She didn't breathe until they stopped.

She left every lamp on in the house.

That night, she dreamed of standing on her porch and seeing her own body out by the mailbox. Just standing there, still and slack. Not moving. Not blinking. She woke to darkness, her clock blinking zeroes.

Outside, the sky had begun to crack.

She woke a second time with a gasp.

It was still dark out. Early, maybe four or five. The sky outside her window was colorless, neither night nor morning. Just a blankness stretching over the tops of the trees.

Hazel dressed without turning on the lights.

She stepped outside and stood in the chill, listening for birds. None. Not even the junk sparrows that nested in her gutters. No wind either. Just the dull ache of stillness, like the town had stopped breathing in the night.

At the diner, only Linda remained.

She was sweeping, over and over, the same patch of

linoleum by the entrance. The counter lights were off. No music. Just the scratch of the broom and the clink of Hazel's keys when she set them down.

"They're all gone," Linda said without turning. "All of them. I unlocked the door at six like always, but no one came."

Hazel sat down at the counter.

"Do you remember that day we helped Georgia and Vince move into the place on Bayshore road?" Hazel asked.

Linda blinked, slowly. "She had that ugly orange couch."

"With the cigarette burns," Hazel said. "Marcy and I couldn't lift it. You just shoved it with your hip like it was a shopping cart."

Linda gave a soft laugh. It was the first time Hazel had heard someone laugh in days. It didn't last long.

They sat in silence for a while. Linda poured them each a cup of coffee from a pot that had long since gone bitter.

Hazel wrapped her hands around the mug like she needed the heat to hold her together.

"I think it's taking us slowly so we notice," Linda said. "So we feel each one."

Hazel didn't answer.

She watched the sun rise behind the empty buildings across the street. Watched the light crawl over a town hollowed out one life at a time.

Later that afternoon, she went to check on Carl.

His chickens were still in the yard, pacing nervously at the edge of the fence. But his boots were on the porch and his truck was still in the drive.

Inside, the radio was playing again.

Only it wasn't music. Just a faint whispering voice, too soft to make out. Hazel leaned in close, turned the dial. The voice stayed there—low, breathy, almost chanting—but she couldn't understand a word.

She turned it off and left the house.

That night, Linda didn't come to the diner.

Hazel called her name from the sidewalk. Waited. Knelt to look under the locked door.

There was no sign of her.

Hazel was alone.

Not metaphorically. Not emotionally. Not in the way you say someone's alone because they lost a loved one or drifted from old friends.

She was alone.

The town was still here. The buildings. The sidewalks. The sky, blank and too quiet. But no cars passed. No dogs barked. No mail came.

She lit candles as the sky dimmed. She did not turn on the radio.

She cooked breakfast the next morning like she had someone to feed. Left a plate across the table. Took small bites. Ate slowly.

And when the sky cracked—soft and clean, as though someone had peeled it open with invisible hands—Hazel closed her eyes and said aloud, "I'm still here."

When she opened them again, the light had changed.

The town was no longer empty.

Hazel stepped out onto her porch.

The morning air was warmer than she remembered. The maple trees in her yard had leaves again—thick green ones that swayed in a wind she couldn't feel. Down the street, cars moved. People walked dogs. A man in a red windbreaker jogged by and waved.

She waved back without thinking. Then froze.

The man was a stranger. His face didn't belong to anyone she remembered, and yet... he wore Marcy's jacket.

Hazel walked into town. The sidewalks had no cracks. The diner windows gleamed like they'd just been installed. The blinking yellow light at Main and Third was gone, replaced by a new stoplight. Red. Then green.

She passed the post office. A young woman with short black hair was sorting mail inside.

Everyone she passed smiled like she was new.

At the market, a cashier said, "Welcome in, ma'am. First time here?"

Hazel nodded.

She bought a loaf of bread. Paid in cash. Her hands trembled slightly as she handed over the bills.

She walked to the overlook before dusk.

The air up there was clearer than it had ever been. The river below shone like metal. The sky stretched out, whole again, unbroken.

Hazel sat on the bench that hadn't been there before. Ran her fingers along its smooth edge.

She could try to ask someone what this place was. Could try to find Linda, or Carl, or Warren. But she knew she wouldn't.

They weren't here. Not anymore.

A soft breeze moved her hair. The sun dipped lower.

Hazel closed her eyes.

She didn't cry.

She didn't smile.

She just stayed there, still, like part of the landscape.

Waiting to see what came next.

Lucy met Anna when they were five, two ponytailed shadows chasing each other across the kindergarten playground. From that day forward, they were rarely apart. Their names were said in a single breath by teachers and parents alike: *LucyandAnna*.

They built kingdoms in the sandbox, whispered secrets in the dark during sleepovers, and made a pact, sealed with cherry lip gloss, that they'd be best friends forever. Every scraped knee, every bad dream, every petty childhood fear was met with the same solemn vow from Anna: *"I've got you."*

By the time they turned ten, they'd written an entire mythology of their friendship. Hand-drawn maps, codes only they understood, even a made-up language spoken through giggles at the lunch table. They had a tree in the park that was *theirs*, a bench behind the school where they'd hide from the world, a pair of matching necklaces with tiny silver stars.

Then Lucy got sick.

It started small. A lingering cold. Fatigue. A low-grade

fever that never seemed to break. Soon, she was missing school. Her room became a quiet island lit by the soft light of her reading lamp and the occasional rustle of her mother's worry.

At first, Anna visited. She brought cards covered in stickers, updates on the latest drama at recess, and promises that things would go back to normal soon.

Then, without explanation, Anna stopped coming.

No more texts. No more drawings taped to the window. When she eventually returned to school and excited to see Anna again, Lucy overheard her laughing with the other girls. Louder now, like Lucy had taken up too much space before and everything was expanding without her.

She tried to pretend it didn't hurt, but it settled in her like a bruise that wouldn't fade. One night, lying awake in the glow of her pink nightlight, she whispered her friend's name into the dark.

The silence answered first.

Then came the voice.

Soft, warm, and impossibly close, rising from the shadows beneath her bed. It was a young girl's voice, although somewhat deeper.

"You don't have to be alone."

She didn't scream. Maybe she was too tired. Maybe some part of her had been waiting for an answer.

Lucy turned slowly toward the edge of her bed, where the shadows thickened between the floorboards.

"Who are you?"

The voice was gentle. *"A friend."*

"I had a friend."

"But she left you."

Lucy looked toward the window, where Anna used to

tap twice on the glass before climbing in. The curtains didn't move. The glass had stayed cold for months.

"She did," Lucy whispered.

"*I won't.*"

Before the quiet settled, the voice had asked just once: "*Will you let me out someday?*" Lucy, still aching, still hollow, had whispered, "Yes."

The voice didn't ask for the promise again that night. It just stayed with her—talking, listening, making her laugh in the quiet hours when the world felt too far away. When she cried, it shushed her. When her stomach hurt and her limbs ached, it distracted her with games: name five things you hate, five things you miss, five things you wish would disappear.

Each time Lucy named "Anna," the voice replied with: "*She already has.*"

By sixth grade, Lucy had stopped hoping her old friend would return. Her illness had eased into something chronic, an undercurrent she carried in her bones. She sat near the window, alone. Anna had drifted into a new orbit of shinier girls with louder laughs.

The voice was always there at the end of the day.

She began to talk to it like she used to talk to Anna. Sometimes aloud, when no one was around. Sometimes just in her mind. It responded with the same dry wit, the same quiet loyalty. It never asked questions it didn't already know the answer to.

She asked once what it looked like.

"*Whatever you need.*"

That summer, when her parents argued downstairs and her stomach curled with the old familiar ache, she whispered, "Can I let you out now?"

The voice hesitated.

"Not yet."

"Why not?"

"Because you're not ready."

She wanted to be ready. She wanted something of her own. Something that would never leave.

By high school, Lucy had learned the art of moving around the edges.

She wasn't unpopular exactly. She was the kind of girl who people remembered sitting near, but not with. She wore knit cardigans in warm weather, drew spirals in the margins of her notes, and always carried a paperback book that she never seemed to read.

When her name was called in class, she'd answer just loud enough to be heard, then vanish again into her chair like smoke. Teachers called her "creative." Her guidance counselor once called her "self-contained," which felt like a nicer word for lonely.

Anna was still there, in the same school, two hallways over. Lucy would sometimes see her at her locker, surrounded by girls in cropped sweatshirts and messy buns, talking over one another like they were afraid of silence. Lucy sometimes saw her laughing near her locker, surrounded by noise. Anna's laugh had changed. Sharper now, edged with something Lucy couldn't name.

She never looked Lucy's way. Not once.

One night, after scrolling through a photo of Anna and her friends at a Halloween party, dressed like stars, arms wrapped around each other, Lucy stared at her screen for a long time. The ache in her chest had no name.

"I want her to know what it's like to be invisible," she whispered.

The voice stirred. *"I could help with that."*

Lucy froze.

"One word. I'll make her feel it. Just like you did."

She didn't say yes. But she didn't say no, either.

She turned off her phone and let the dark hold her. In the morning, she felt sick with herself.

"I think something's wrong with me," she whispered.

"There's nothing wrong with you," the voice replied. *"You're just keeping your promise."*

Through it all, the voice remained her constant. It didn't ask questions. It didn't change.

It waited.

Lucy joined clubs she didn't care about: the school newspaper, the art club, the recycling committee that never really recycled anything. She sat in circles, nodded when it felt appropriate, and practiced small smiles in the bathroom mirror. She even tried joining a conversation about someone's party, though the words felt like pebbles in her mouth.

That night, she cried into her pillow and whispered, "I think I'm getting worse."

"You're getting stronger," the voice said from beneath her bed.

"You're learning how to live without pretending she'll ever come back."

She buried her face in the blankets. "I don't want to be strong. I just want—"

She didn't finish.

"You just want it to stop hurting."

"Yes."

"One day, it will. You'll keep your promise. And everything will change."

Sometimes, Lucy wrote letters she never sent. To Anna. To herself. To something she imagined living in the space between them. She folded them into origami and dropped them down the vent behind her dresser.

One read: *I miss the way I used to laugh.*

Another: *Was I too much? Or not enough?*

The voice never mocked her for these. It would murmur softly in the dark: *"She never deserved you."*

On harder nights, it would hum lullabies that sounded like songs from her childhood, just slightly wrong, off-key and cracked like they came from underwater.

Lucy once dated a boy named Evan for three weeks. He had freckles and wrote songs on a busted ukulele. She liked his weird, wandering thoughts and the way he sat too close when he got excited.

The voice went quiet during that time.

Then Evan told her she was "hard to read."

That she "held things back."

That he didn't know if she even *liked* him.

The voice came back before the door had clicked shut behind him.

"You tried. He left. Just like her."

Lucy curled up under her blanket, face hot with shame.

"Is there something wrong with me?"

"There's nothing wrong with you."

"You're just keeping your promise."

Through it all, the voice remained her constant. It didn't ask questions. It didn't change.

It waited.

And sometimes, when she lay awake with her feet dangling slightly off the bed, she could feel the faintest pressure—like someone resting their hand lightly on her ankle. Not menacing. Just... there.

A reminder.

College felt like the world had been wiped clean. New people, new buildings, new routines.

Lucy took to it quietly, like slipping into a coat that

almost fit. She double-majored in psychology and literature. Sat in the same seat for every class. Bought coffee from the same grumpy barista who learned her name by October. Her roommate was a theater major named Talia who talked with her hands and had a laugh like wind chimes in a thunderstorm.

Talia liked Lucy. Called her "mysterious." Invited her to open mics, film clubs, tarot readings in the dorm basement. Lucy went, sometimes. She even let herself enjoy it.

The voice didn't disappear. But it thinned, like mist in a back room she kept locked. Sometimes she'd hear it when she couldn't sleep, its tone thoughtful, almost distant.

"They don't really see you."

She'd whisper back, "Maybe they don't have to. Maybe it's enough that I'm here."

"Yes."

By December, campus emptied out. Lucy rode a cramped bus back to her hometown, watching frost form spiderwebs on the window. Her neighborhood looked smaller, like a model version of itself. The streets felt heavier somehow, more memories in the pavement than cars.

Her childhood bedroom was mostly untouched. Same old posters, the dusty bookshelf, the soft hum of the vent that always sounded like whispering.

The voice stayed with her the first night back.

"We're home again."

"I'm not staying long," she said, unpacking.

"It's nice being back."

Three days into break, Lucy ran into Anna at the local bookstore.

She almost didn't recognize her at first. Anna had dyed her hair darker and cut it shoulder-length. She wore a vintage army jacket and thick-rimmed glasses. Her laugh hadn't changed, though, it still had that upward lilt at the end, like she was always about to say something funny.

Lucy was about to turn away when Anna spotted her.

"Oh...Lucy?"

They both froze. Lucy's mouth felt full of snow.

Anna smiled, uncertain. "Hey."

"Hi."

A silence stretched. Then Anna gestured at the shelf. "They still carry these? Remember those awful fairy books we used to read?"

Lucy nodded. "You made me pretend I was the pixie queen."

"You *were* the pixie queen," Anna said, laughing. Then her smile dimmed. "It's been a long time."

"It has."

Another pause. Then, softer: "I...I'm sorry I didn't come around. Back then."

Lucy felt her stomach drop. The moment felt too narrow for all the things she wanted to say.

She managed a tight smile. "It's okay."

Anna nodded, chewing her bottom lip. "I think about it more than I should."

Lucy wanted to ask why. Why she vanished. Why she never said anything. Why she acted like Lucy had just... stopped existing.

But instead, she said, "It's good to see you."

"You too," Anna said. "Merry Christmas."

Lucy watched her leave. The bell above the door jingled like it was laughing.

That night, she lay in bed, staring at the ceiling. The voice crept back in like a cold draft.

"She left you because you were broken."

"Don't," Lucy whispered.

"Face the truth. You were sick. You scared her. She couldn't even look at you."

"I don't want to do this again."

"Then set me free."

She turned her face into the pillow.

The floor creaked beneath her bed. A soft knock.

Then another.

Like knuckles rapping on wood from the inside out.

She didn't sleep the night she saw Anna.

Even when she closed her eyes, Lucy kept replaying the bookstore: the careful words, the space between them, the almost. Anna's voice still lived somewhere inside her, like a favorite song she didn't know was still stuck in her head.

The voice beneath the bed didn't speak that night. But she felt it. Not as sound, but as presence, like someone standing just behind her shoulder in a mirror.

Back at college, the stillness followed her. The voice had grown quieter, but its silence no longer felt restful. It was like waiting for thunder after the lightning had already struck.

She felt it again at dusk, just as the campus lights blinked on outside her dorm window.

Tap.

A pause.

Tap.

Lucy sat on the floor of her room, knees drawn to her chest. The shoebox she had brought from home was in her lap, faded notes, ticket stubs, the silver star necklace missing its chain.

She pulled out a page she hadn't touched in years. A letter she wrote to Anna when she was twelve, but never sent.

The handwriting was round and hopeful.

Dear Anna,

Why did you stop being my friend? I think I got weird. Or too sad. But you never even said why. I still keep looking for you in the hallways. I don't know how to make this go away.

Lucy pressed the letter to her chest, then folded it and laid it on the floor beside her.

She reached for her journal and, after a long pause, wrote something new:

Dear Anna,

I wanted to tell you that I missed you.

I didn't know how much until I saw you again.

I spent years being angry at you. At myself. I thought if I forgave you, it would mean what you did was okay.

But I think now, we were just girls.

And I was sick.

And you were scared.

And maybe we both didn't know what to do.

So this is me saying it out loud:

I forgive you.

Not because you asked me to.

But because I want to be free.

—Lucy

She sat with that for a long time.

Then she stood, walked to the small mail slot in her dorm's hallway, and dropped it through.

That night, the knock returned.

This time, not tentative. Not shy.

Three steady raps beneath her bed.

"You waited a long time," she whispered.

The voice answered, soft as breath: *"You made a promise."*

"I did."

She slipped to the floor. Got on her hands and knees. Leaned down and lifted the edge of the blanket, revealing the shadowed space beneath.

It was empty.

Just quiet and dust.

Still, she crawled closer. Reached in. Touched the wood of the far wall. Then she lay flat on the floor, her cheek against the ground, arms stretched outward. Her body a bridge between then and now.

The sob rose from somewhere deep. The kind of sob that unspooled everything...grief, memory, shame, love. She cried without holding it in. For Anna. For herself. For the girl who kept it all buried.

No voice came to comfort her this time.

Just the sound of her own breath.

Eventually, she turned onto her back, still on the floor. Staring up at the ceiling. The room was the same, but she was not.

In the quiet that followed, she felt something loosen inside her—not leave, but *unclench*. Like a hand that had been balled into a fist for too long finally opening.

"I'm letting you out," she whispered. "Not because I'm afraid. Not because I owe you. But because I don't need you anymore."

That night, Lucy didn't turn on the lamp.

She sat on the floor of her room, shoebox beside her, her journal open but untouched. The letter to Anna was gone, mailed, without ceremony or return address. There was nothing else to do. Nothing else to say.

Only the waiting.

She slid down onto her side, curled where the floor met the bed frame. The carpet was cool against her skin. She closed her eyes.

Three soft knocks came from beneath her.

Not angry. Not desperate.

Just steady.

I'm still here, they seemed to say.

Lucy didn't answer. Not aloud.

Instead, she reached beneath the bed, expecting what? A hand? A shape in the dark? But there was nothing. Only stillness. The quiet held her like a blanket. And for the first time in her life, she didn't fear the quiet.

She lay there a long time, not asleep but somewhere near it. The knocks didn't come again.

The voice didn't speak.

Whatever had been waiting was done waiting.

She stayed on the floor until morning, her old friend finally quiet.

And for once, the silence didn't ache.

The knocking never came again. But the promise had been kept.

THE ROAD HAD VANISHED miles ago. What remained was a suggestion of direction, two faint wheel ruts swallowed by ferns and damp earth. Lawrence guided the vintage Blazer through the underbrush, branches whispering against the windows, the sky overhead a dull smear of gray. He had expected solitude, but not this kind of forgetting...the land seemed uninterested in being remembered.

When the cabin finally emerged through the trees, it looked more like something discovered than rented. Squat and dark, its timbers softened by moss and age, it stood with the quiet patience of a place long unbothered by human needs.

He turned off the engine and sat for a moment. The ticking of the cooling truck filled the silence. No phone towers, no hum of highways, no other cabins tucked nearby. He'd wanted remote, and he had found it. Still, something in him shrank.

Inside, the cabin was cleaner than he expected. Sparse furniture, thick rugs faded by sun, a wood stove crouched in the corner. He unpacked slowly: laptop, notebooks, a small stack of paperbacks he wouldn't read. His wife had tucked in a thermos of coffee and a sandwich wrapped in wax paper. She always knew how to love him, even when she didn't understand him. He hated how heavy that made him feel.

There was nothing wrong with his life, and that was the worst part.

Two kids, both still young enough to think he was strong. A house in a good school district. A job in marketing that paid better than it deserved. And a sadness that moved through him like fog...impossible to hold, but always there.

He'd come to the woods to write, or at least, that was the excuse. He didn't know what he was hoping to find. Maybe the right words would name the thing inside him. Maybe naming it would help.

The first day passed in stillness.He set up his laptop on the old oak table, drank coffee that tasted like burnt pine, and wrote half a paragraph about a man walking into the woods. He deleted it. He walked the perimeter of the clearing, feeling foolish as he looked for snakes. A hawk circled once overhead and vanished. He typed a few lines that went nowhere. Deleted them. Read the first ten pages of a book about grief and closed it before the author's name had even settled.

That night, the fire in the stove burned low. He let it. He liked the cold, the way it made him feel closer to something real. The quiet pressed in like a second skin.

That night, as wind sifted through the trees and the moon dragged shadows across the floorboards, he heard it.

A pause in the silence. A rhythm.

Scrape. Pause. Thump.

It came from the trees beyond the cabin. The sound of a

shovel, methodical and steady. Not frantic. Not careless. Just… workmanlike.

He held his breath. Moved to the window and peered out into the black. The porch light cast a narrow cone over the steps and the bare edge of the treeline, but beyond that —nothing. Just darkness layered on darkness.

The sound stopped.

He waited for it to begin again. It didn't.

Eventually, he climbed into bed, unsure if he was more disturbed that it happened, or that it hadn't.

He woke early, with a dry mouth and a cramp in his neck from sleeping sideways on too many pillows. The stove had gone cold. Frost feathered the window glass. For a moment, he forgot where he was.

Then the night came back to him, not as memory but as mood. That strange quiet with something behind it. The sound of digging. Real or not, it lingered like the smell of smoke in fabric.

Lawrence poured the coffee his wife had sent. It was lukewarm, metallic. He drank it anyway, bundled himself into a jacket, and stepped outside. The air was brittle, holding the smell of sap and frozen leaves. The trees stood still.

He walked to the edge of the clearing, past the rusted pump and the stump that looked too cleanly cut to be recent. He scanned the ground for signs—disruption, foot-prints, a displaced stone.

There was nothing.

He pushed further into the woods, navigating between the trees where needles softened the earth and shadows stayed even in morning light. He listened for birds, for small creatures stirring. But the forest held its breath.

After twenty minutes of searching, he circled back. No

hole. No shovel. Just the trees, watching in their slow, patient way.

Back in the cabin, he tried to write. But the page stayed white, and the white grew unbearable. He wrote a line and erased it. Then another. Something about winter and forgetting, but it sounded cheap. Like it belonged on a mug.

By afternoon, a dull headache had begun to bloom behind his eyes. He lay down and let it take him.

When he woke, it was near dusk. The light had gone syrupy, golden in the tops of the trees, and bruised near the ground. He went outside again, walking the clearing with his arms wrapped around his ribs as if he could hold himself together.

The silence was back. But it wasn't empty. It was full of listening.

That night, the shovel came again.

It started just after midnight, faint and distant, like a memory rising from deep beneath the floorboards.

Scrape. Pause. Thump.

Always in threes. Always the same.

This time, Lawrence didn't go to the window. He just lay in bed and listened, heart ticking faster than the rhythm of the sound. He wanted to call out. To ask *who's there?* or *what do you want?*

But part of him already knew.

It wasn't someone. It was something.

And it was digging for him.

Lawrence didn't sleep much the third night. He stayed in bed with the covers pulled to his chest, listening to every creak of the cabin. His heartbeat had taken on the rhythm of the digging: scrape, pause, thump. Only it wasn't there. Not that night. That absence, somehow, was worse.

He woke to the pale light of morning and a weight

pressing on his chest—not physical, but constant, like guilt that had forgotten its origin. He didn't go outside. He couldn't.

Instead, he paced the floor. Made instant oatmeal and didn't eat it. Jotted thoughts in a notebook: half a sentence about a man in a well, then a sketch of a hand reaching up from soil. He flipped the page and wrote, *Something is wrong with me,* then scribbled over it until the paper tore.

He hadn't told anyone the real reason he came here. Not even Emily. She thought it was a writing retreat, his way of chasing the novel he'd always talked about. The one he joked about at dinner parties but never started. He'd told her the time away would help.

What he hadn't told her was that he cried in the car some mornings for no reason. That he stared at his kids too long and wondered how long he could fake being whole. That when he laughed, it didn't feel like him. Just something wearing his face.

The forest outside looked still, but it wasn't. It pulsed. Not in movement, but in presence. He started keeping the curtains closed.

On the fourth day, he heard voices in the static of the wind. Not words, just the tone of conversation. Like two people talking through a wall. He went out onto the porch and stood barefoot in the cold, listening. There was only wind. Only trees.

But he didn't feel alone.

That evening, he sat at the table and stared at the blank laptop screen for hours. The glow of it made his eyes ache. He turned it off.

Later, in the dark, he whispered out loud:

"Please stop."

The digging began again.

This time, it was closer.

Scrape. Pause. Thump.

It wasn't faint now. It was just beyond the porch. Maybe ten feet past the treeline.

Lawrence sat rigid in the dark, hands gripping the edge of the mattress. His breath came shallow. His body wanted to move, to run, but there was nowhere to go. He pictured stepping outside and seeing a figure with its back to him, lifting and plunging a shovel into the ground. Again. And again.

He didn't go to the window.

Instead, he curled beneath the covers, knees drawn up, heart trying to claw its way out of his chest.

The sound continued for what felt like hours, then stopped mid-thump. Like it had heard his thoughts.

He didn't sleep. Not at all.

And when light finally touched the world again, he stepped outside with trembling hands.

The clearing looked the same.

The pump. The stump. The damp smell of pine.

But now... something else.

A shovel. Leaning against the nearest tree.

Its blade was wet with earth.

The shovel stood like it had been placed with care. Not dropped, not forgotten. Planted. Its wooden handle pale and smooth, as if polished by many hands. The blade was caked in black soil, damp and clotted, the kind that came from deeper down where worms curled and roots grew blind.

Lawrence stared at it for a long time, unmoving. A draft stirred behind him. The cabin door, still open. The inside calling him back. He didn't go. He stepped forward.

Each footfall felt like a trespass.

He followed the direction the shovel faced, past the nearest trees, into the thinning underbrush. About thirty feet in, the leaves gave way to raw earth. Not a clearing. Not natural.

A pit.

Roughly six feet long. Maybe three wide. Its sides were sharp, its corners squared off. Not animal work. Not erosion.

Someone had dug it. Recently. Carefully.

He stood at its edge, his breath fogging in the cold air. A crow called in the distance… harsh and singular.

He waited for the thud of his own heartbeat to pass. Then he crouched beside the hole, ran his hand just over the soil. Loose clumps, fresh. The bottom was uneven, like whoever had dug it was interrupted.

Or planning to return.

Lawrence tried to swallow, but his throat felt thick. The smell rising from the pit was not rot, not yet, but it was heavy. Earth that had been undisturbed for a long time. Like opening a wound.

He whispered, "No."

Then louder: "No."

His voice fell into the woods and didn't echo.

The digging hadn't just happened. It had accumulated. Night after night. And this—this was what it had been building toward. Methodical. Measured. The sound wasn't madness. It was progress.

He stood up and looked around. The forest didn't respond.

Still, something in him moved, a slow churning, like the start of nausea. Or a realization too big to hold all at once.

The grave was empty. But it felt claimed.

He stumbled back toward the cabin, limbs cold and stiff, pulse hammering in his ears.

Back inside, he locked the door. Not that it mattered. The lock was small. The windows were thin.

He sat at the table. The cursor on his laptop blinked like a pulse.

This is for me, he typed.

Then deleted it.

He put the kettle on, hands shaking, and watched the steam curl upward. His reflection in the window didn't look like him. Pale. Eyes too dark. Or maybe the light just caught wrong.

He turned away from it. Sat down. Tried to breathe deeply.

And outside, just beneath the hush of wind through branches, came a new sound.

Faint. Rhythmic.

Scrape. Pause. Thump.

He didn't go back outside.

Not that day. Not the next.

He kept the fire going and moved through the cabin like a shadow of himself. Ate when he remembered. Slept when exhaustion pinned him. But mostly, he sat at the table and stared at the door—waiting for a knock that wouldn't come. Or for the sound of footsteps in the leaves.

None came.

Just the shovel. Night after night. He could hear it before it began—like his body was tuned to it.

Scrape. Pause. Thump.

It had become a rhythm in his chest. A second heart-beat. Familiar. Almost intimate.

He started writing again, but not fiction.

He wrote lists.

- Things I remember loving

- Places I felt real

- What I would say to my kids if I left

And then, without intending to:

- What would they say about me at my funeral?

He didn't cry. He hadn't cried in years. It was like his body had burned through its sadness and left something dry and hollow in its place. He read over the last list again and again, thinking of how little he'd let himself be known.

Emily would say he was thoughtful. The kids might say he was funny. His coworkers would say *quiet, but steady*—a phrase meant to praise, but always felt like dismissal.

He wondered if the forest had listened to all that silence inside him and decided to give it shape.

Wasn't that what the pit was?

The shape of something wordless.

Not a threat, but an echo.

He stood at the window and watched the wind comb through the trees. The shovel was still there, leaning as it had been. The grave too, waiting. No animals disturbed it. No storm had softened its edges.

It was a constant. Like his sadness.

Like the thought, never voiced, that the world might move easier without him in it.

He sat back down.

Typed slowly:

What if the hole isn't to bury me—

but to show me what I've been digging all along?

He stared at it for a long time. Then he closed the laptop.

The fire cracked. The kettle whistled. Somewhere far off, a raven cried once, and was gone.

That night, he didn't wait for the digging.

He dressed in layers, lit a lantern, and stepped outside before the sound began. The air was still. Cold. The kind that settles into the joints and makes you feel older than you are.

The forest didn't resist him. It welcomed him now, or maybe it had simply accepted him.

The shovel was where he left it.

He picked it up.

His hands closed around the wood and found it familiar. Not menacing. Just a tool. A thing made for work.

He walked to the pit.

It hadn't grown deeper, but it felt changed, more defined, like its presence had sharpened. It didn't look like a grave tonight. It looked like a mirror.

He stood at the edge and stared into it.

Not to measure it. Not to imagine himself inside it.

Just... to see it.

The hole had always been there, hadn't it? Inside him.

Dug slowly over years. By routine. By silence. By the feeling that joy had to be earned.

But he had never looked straight at it before.

He knelt and touched the rim of the soil, fingers pressing into the cold earth. It didn't recoil. It just gave a little. Accepted him.

He thought about his lists. About the laughter of his children, the way Emily always kissed his shoulder when passing behind him in the kitchen. The time he stayed up all night to build a cardboard fort. The way his daughter whispered, *You're safe now,* when he tucked her in.

All of it.

He whispered, "I'm still here."

Not to the trees. Not to the dark.

To himself.

The wind moved. Just slightly. As if in answer.

He placed the shovel in the pit, gently, like laying down a burden. Then stood. And stepped back.

The forest made no sound.

But something lifted.

He didn't need to fill the hole tonight. That could come later.

What mattered was that he had seen it and didn't climb in.

<hr>

The kitchen was full of late afternoon light, the kind that turned everything amber and soft around the edges. Lawrence stood at the counter slicing apples, listening to the kettle begin its low hiss.

His daughter sat at the table, drawing with serious concentration, green marker smudged across her knuckles.

His son was on the floor nearby, building towers from mismatched blocks and knocking them over with exaggerated groans.

The noise wasn't overwhelming today. It filled the room like warmth.

Emily leaned against the doorway, her arms crossed loosely, watching him in that way she did when she wasn't sure what to ask.

"You doing okay?" she said gently.

He looked up and smiled... not wide, but real. The kind that used to feel like a lie, now worn with honesty.

"Yeah," he said. "I think I am."

He still had quiet days. Still felt the slow undertow pulling at the corners of things. But it didn't scare him anymore.

He'd seen the shape of it. Touched its edges. And understood that it didn't want to bury him.

It wanted him to notice.

To feel the weight of his life not as a burden, but as proof that it existed. That *he* existed. That the depth in him wasn't something to escape, but to live from.

Sometimes, when the house was still and the windows open, he thought he could hear the echo of that old rhythm in the back of his mind.

Scrape. Pause. Thump.

But now, it felt like something different.

Like a heartbeat.

Like someone, somewhere, building their way back to the surface.

I didn't set out to write horror. I set out to write about the quiet things that haunt us.

Static Between the Trees is a collection of stories shaped by silence, by the moments that don't make headlines but stay with you anyway. The absence of a friend. The weight of an unspoken goodbye. The strange way memory shifts like fog over time.

These stories take place in small towns and wooded spaces, but more than that, they live in the hollow between what we say and what we mean. Some are unsettling. Some are surreal. All of them come from the same place: the still space between the trees.

Thank you for walking into the woods with me.
— N.B. Cross

N.B. Cross writes quiet horror and dark fiction rooted in small towns, haunted landscapes, and the shadows that live between memory and grief. His short story collection, Static Between the Trees, introduced readers to his blend of atmosphere and unease. Hollow Stone is the first book in the Stonebound Trilogy.

Learn more at nbcrossauthor.com and join the Hollow newsletter (if you haven't already) for a free story and upcoming announcements.

 instagram.com/n.b.cross
 facebook.com/nbcrossauthor

Coming November 2025: Hollow Stone (Stonebound Book 1)

Coming December 2025: Quiet Bloom (Stonebound Book 2)

9 781970 425048